THE WENTWORTH TRIPLETS
MYSTERY SERIES

VOLUME 3

THE CASE OF THE HOLLOW HILL

THE CASE OF THE TUMBLING TRIPLET

JOANN KLUSMEYER

innovo
PUBLISHING

Published by Innovo Publishing, LLC
www.innovopublishing.com
1-888-546-2111

Providing Full-Service Publishing Services for Christian Authors, Artists &
Ministries: Books, eBooks, Audiobooks, Music, Screenplays, Film & Curricula

**THE WENTWORTH TRIPLETS
MYSTERY SERIES
FOR YOUNG TEENS**

Volume 3

**THE CASE OF THE HOLLOW HILL
&
THE CASE OF THE TUMBLING TRIPLET**

ISBN: 978-1-61314-656-9

Cover Design & Interior Layout: Innovo Publishing, LLC

Printed in the United States of America
U.S. Printing History
First Edition: 2021

Has God called you to create a Christian book, ebook, audiobook, music album,
screenplay, film, or curricula? If so, visit the ChristianPublishingPortal.com to
learn how to accomplish your calling with excellence. Learn to do everything
yourself, or hire trusted Christian Experts from our Marketplace to help.

CONTENTS

A NOTE FROM THE PUBLISHER

Although the Wentworth triplets are fictional, the models depicting them on the back cover are real triplets (Aden, Cole & Eva Claire) who, at the time, were the same age as the characters. Just like the fictional Wentworths, the real triplets and their parents are believers. And if that wasn't coincidence enough, the real dad is a world-traveling pilot just like his fictional counterpart. Interestingly, the author didn't know the models or their family. What are the odds? At Innovo we like to say, "With God—one hundred percent!"

THE CASE OF THE HOLLOW HILL

W hat's the name of that place? Tell me again, Dad," Darla Wentworth asked, studying the map spread out before her.

"Independence Pass. Don't you ever listen?" came the ungracious reply of her brother, Danny.

"Thanks, but you aren't Dad, remember?" Darla reminded him.

"How long will we be gone, Dad?" questioned Dennis, the third member of the Wentworth triplets.

"Two weeks," answered Darla.

Montgomery Wentworth, father of the thirteen-year-old triplets, sat reading the sports page of the newspaper. He almost never answered their questions without pausing for a minute. His children had been answering each other for him since they were eight or nine years old, and now, at thirteen, what one of them didn't hear or understand, another one of them usually did. If he waited, they usually answered their own questions. Actually, he had enough to think of when the family went on these trips. There was the helicopter that must be serviced, camping rations to be arranged for, and most importantly, the cameras must be checked out and made ready. The cameras, of course, were the reason for making the trip.

This was not just a camping trip in which they only hoped for good weather. In fact, a good solid shower of rain would be welcome. Not that they wanted to get wet, but the photographer had an assignment to produce a documentary film on a mountain watershed. He would be searching for an area on the continental divide in

Colorado, where a drop of water that fell to the ground could almost have a choice of flowing to the west, toward the Pacific Ocean, or going east into the Mississippi River and then into the Gulf of Mexico. He would be looking for a spot on the mountain pass where something like that could occur.

Darla spread out the photographs that her father had taken earlier to show to the people who were buying the film so they could decide where they wanted the film to be made. The pictures were of tree tops, mountain tops and piles of rocks. There were bluffs and solid walls of gray rocks with small, scrubby trees hanging to the cliffs, with bare roots that fingered their tentacles into rock crevasses, searching for nutrients.

"Look, Dad. There's a pointed hill. Let's land the chopper on that one and see what the view is from up there," Darla requested.

Danny leaned over Darla's shoulder. "We couldn't land on that. It's not flat enough. The propeller would hit all those rocks."

Dennis leaned over her other shoulder.

"Wouldn't either. It's bigger than it looks to be in the picture. See the size of those trees over there?"

"Naw, those are just little trees."

"Then see that bare spot there? That's plenty of room to set down the chopper."

"Is not. Look at that cliff right there."

Darla had ducked down and eased away, and her brothers moved in closer to the photos. Dennis insisted, "How big do you think that chopper is, anyway? Why, Dad could land it on a ping-pong table."

"Maybe so, but there isn't a ping-pong table down there. The mountain is too little and pointed."

Dad kept reading.

Darla sighed. She was not as excited about this trip as she usually was because their cousin, Sally Copelan, could not come along with them on this trip. A stupid piano recital was destroying her fun, and in addition to all of that, Darla was not going to be able to go to the recital to hear Sally play her piano piece.

Sometimes nothing came out right. Even when you had prayed and when you had given God a lot of time to work things out. Darla hoped that was important. She folded her jeans and heavy shirts, her thick socks and heavy boots. Dad didn't have to remind her that the mountains got very cold, even in June, and that she must take boots or there was a risk of a sprained ankle.

She packed the mosquito repellant and the sunscreen, the sewing kit and the scissors. Yes, she knew exactly what to take. From the top of the closet she got down the insulated coveralls she slept in during mountain camping trips. She set out the hammock which was made to hook onto the inside walls of the chopper to make enough beds. She slept in the chopper while Dad and the boys took the tent. The hammock she used was a double one, big enough for Sally to share it with her, but on this trip there would be no Sally.

Darla laid out her rain slicker and boots. Who could guess whether it would rain, but it probably would not rain on this trip because they were hoping it would. Things sometimes worked out that way.

Dad stepped into her room and looked around at the assorted gear lined up against the wall. It nearly filled the tiny room. Mobile home bedrooms were not exceptionally large, and she had the biggest of the four, but it was still quite small and cramped in comparison to her "winter" bedroom at their grandparents' house.

Dad looked around the room, and then he looked at her. "You're not really excited about this trip, are you, Kitten?"

"I would be, Dad, if only Sally could come. I prayed about it and I prayed about it, but God didn't answer. I don't think He heard."

"Of course He heard. He hears us the first time we pray, but sometimes we just don't like the answers He gives."

"But, Dad, why did that stinking old piano recital have to be now?"

"We mustn't question God, Kitten. The reason I came in was to ask you if you would like to stay here this time. Then you could go to the recital with Sally. She would like that a lot."

"Oh, could I?" Then she thought, "But, Dad, you know how much I like the mountains. I really want to go, but...."

Dad smiled at her dilemma. "You'll have to decide. It will give you practice on being a grownup. They are always having to decide the best of two good things and the least bad of two bad things, so you just think about it and let me know." Then Dad left her room.

"I guess I'll stay," Darla told the walls of her room, "but I really want to go. So I'll go. But it won't be much fun without Sally along." To go? Or to stay! Which? By now Darla was so tired she quit thinking and packing and went to bed.

Through the walls of the mobile, Darla could hear her brothers shouting to each other as they packed their gear.

"Do you have my rubber boot?"

"No, I have only two boots."

"But are they for the same foot? Mine are both rights."

"Both rights? That's weird."

"Take a look at yours."

"Oh, yeah. They're both lefts."

Darla couldn't sleep, so she thought some more. To go? Or to stay! Which? "God, I asked you about this a long time ago, and You had time to get everything fixed. Sally asked You, too." Darla sniffed loudly, feeling very sorry for herself. She might as well just stay home because she hadn't gotten everything packed anyway. She was too tired from all the thinking, and Dad was leaving very early in the morning.

Darla took a deep breath, punched her pillow into softness and turned over on her side. She pulled her spare pillow over her head to block out the sounds made by Dennis and Danny. The pillow even blotted out the sound of the telephone that rang directly after the 10:00 o'clock news and weather.

The photographer spoke into the phone. "Hello... Oh, yes, we're just about ready... Yes, I did notice the long range forcast. If the rain came on in from the coast the way they think it might... Yes, I agree. A day of good shooting before a storm, then during and after the showers should produce what we're looking for... Yes, thank you for calling. We'll wait here for two days. That should work out very well... Goodnight."

Danny and Dennis were watching him as he hung up the phone. Dad told them, "Hold up the packing, boys. We're postponed for two days."

"Really?" Dennis said. "Is it going to rain?"

"The weatherman thinks there's a chance."

"So, now Sally can come," remembered Danny. "I'll go tell Darla."

"No," Dad stopped him. "She's asleep. Morning will be soon enough."

Darla opened her eyes as the sun shone into the window on her face. The house was quiet and the only sound was the singing of the birds in the trees overhead.

"They're gone," she told herself. "They didn't even wake me up to say goodbye. But why didn't I wake up? The boys always drop something or stumble into the walls in the mornings. What happened?"

Darla reached for her hairbrush and began to remove the nighttime tangles from her long, taffy-colored hair. The row of camping gear was still leaning against the wall. That would have to be put away as soon as she got up. Then she'd have to call someone to take her over to Sally's house.

Darla twisted her hair up on the top of her head and fastened it with a clamp. She decided a glass of chocolate milk would be nice before she got started putting the stuff away. She slid out of bed and opened her bedroom door. Immediately, she smelled coffee. Huh oh, Dad forgot to unplug the coffeepot! Lucky she was here to take care of it, and she went down the hall to the kitchen to tend to the coffee pot.

"Hello, Kitten."

Darla jumped, startled. "Dad! You've already gone!"

"Have I?" Dad asked, raising his eyebrows.

"Aw, Dad, you know what I mean. It's going to rain later, isn't it? That's why you're still here. We're waiting for the rain. I've got to call Sally and tell her."

"Yes, and you might apologize to God, too, for misjudging Him."

"Oops, you're right, Dad. I will!"

The recital came and went. Sally made no mistakes, at least that anyone could tell, but she was very nervous and sweaty before it was over. Everyone was relieved to have it behind them.

Then it was time to pack the camping gear again. This was an unusually long trip for a helicopter, all the way from Branson, Missouri to the Denver, Colorado area. Ordinarily they would have taken their small airplane, but there were reasons why they couldn't. There was no airport near to where they could rent a chopper, and there would be a lot of scenes to be photographed along the way. Helicopters could set down anywhere, and jet airplanes needed runways. They would have to pack very light, but then, how much stuff would you want to take along on a trip into the mountains like this one?

The suitcases were fitted into the helicopter so they would do double duty as benches. The tent was strapped onto the wall so it would not be flung about. The engine was checked for oil and gas, and the food crates were stowed away. Now everyone, the four Wentworths plus Sally, went back to the mobile to get a good night's sleep.

It was still dark when the five of them drove to the Branson airport, parked the car and boarded the chopper. The propeller whistled as it rotated though the air and the passengers could feel the huge machine lifting them off the ground.

They flew over Table Rock Lake, an inky patch of black with twinkles of light around the edge, pinpointing the boats of the early morning fishermen.

By the time they flew over Cassville, Missouri, the sun was beaming through the trees on the eastern horizon. They flew south of Neosho, Missouri, and then into northeastern Oklahoma. The Grand Lake of the Cherokee was a large, blue quilt with a white fringe around it.

Night darkness found them at Lamar, Colorado, and they had done a lot of "river following" to decide which would be the best shots for the film.

By noon the next day, they were in the mountains, looking down on valleys and mountain tops and on treetops and small streams. It was hard to find a place large enough for the chopper to light. There was hardly a spot that was level enough or was not thickly covered with trees.

At Independence Pass, they began to climb higher, following the "backbone" of the mountain. From the air, it looked as though some giant child had scooped up a ridge of dirt piles and had poked millions of trees into it. Darla and Sally brought out the pictures and began comparing the mountains below them to the ones in the photographs.

"Are you sure these are the right pictures?" Sally asked.

"Positive," insisted Darla.

"But they all look alike. There are all greenish in the valley, but the farther away the mountains are, the bluer the tops are."

"Just look for the pointed mountain," Dennis told her.

"Pointed mountain? Where?"

Dennis held up the photo. "That's the easiest one to identify. That's where we're going."

But things look very different when one is hanging out in space between the mountains. It was sort of like a bird's eye view made to confuse humans and make all mountains look the same. The chopper was like a very big bird looking for a place to light. Below them, actual eagles swooped and the shiny black wings of vultures and crows were dark moving dots.

"Yuck! I hate vultures. They eat old, dead stuff," Danny observed.

Dennis couldn't resist the comment, "Do you eat your meat alive? Besides, vultures only help clean up the bodies of animals that die. Don't they, Dad?"

"So do wolves and wildcats," Danny put in.

"I see it," squealed Sally.

"See what?"

"The mountain. See, right there?"

"Wait, it's not pointed enough."

"But there is that one beside it that is flat on top. The pointed one should be there beside it."

"Yeah, well, I don't know... Dad?"

The helicopter was flying lower now, and the trees became very plain. Old crow's nests dotted the tops of the trees, and here and there were other trees that had broken apart by lightning. Small mountain streams seemed to burst forth from the sides of the steep peaks and rush to the valley to join the rippling, blue river.

"It's gone, Dad," Darla said.

"What's gone?" asked Dennis.

"But where could a mountain go?" Sally wondered.

"But it has to be beside the big one, doesn't it?"

"But it isn't."

"But this is the right place to be."

"How do you know so much?"

"Dad is setting the chopper down. That's how I know."

The helicopter swung around and settled on top of the large, flat rock near the top of a high hill.

"Here we are," announced Mr. Wentworth. "Dennis and Danny, tie down the chopper and set up the tent. Darla and Sally, untie the lanterns and flashlights and get out the stove. You girls have first kitchen duty. Hook up the hammock and locate the food. Dennis, go get a pail of water from that stream and bring it to me, and Danny, you help me carry the tripod to the top of the hill. I want to get some shooting done before the sun goes down."

The chopper came to a stop, and he opened the door.

"Kitten, hand me that case and the other one over there. Now everyone, move fast and make like a bunny rabbit." That meant get busy and do no arguing. When Dad gave orders like that, he had everyone scattering like leaves before a whirlwind. There was a good reason to hurry, as there were no light switches on the trees and no street lights lighting up the mountain. There was no TV, stove or refrigerator. Whatever was to be done after dark must be prepared for while it was still light.

Dennis twisted the long corkscrew tether rods into the ground around the outside of the rock and tied the chopper securely to them with strong ropes. He pulled the ropes extra tight so the mountain wind would not topple the helicopter over on its side and into the valley, no matter how hard it blew.

Dennis was setting up the tent and also tethering it securely to the ground. The tent was made of insulated, waterproof canvas, and the sides zipped together tightly to keep out the cold. It had a floor attached to it so that water from a rain shower would not run under the edges and soak the bedrolls.

The stove with its little cans of fuel was set up on the rock, and Darla and Sally decided on the dinner menu. What would it be? Spaghetti or soup? Spaghetti was nice, but it was rather bad about scorching on the bottom of the kettle unless it was stirred all the time. Soup, on the other hand, could be left on its own for short periods of time. They decided on soup.

They opened one can of wieners and cut them into little "pennies" and added three cans of sloppy joe mix. Now a can of corn and one of green beans. A huge handful of onion flakes and a big pinch of mixed soup spices. How about carrots? Sure, throw them in.

They stirred the vegetables into the meat mix. Was it enough? Everyone was really hungry. Better throw in two cans of tomatoes and a can of tiny potatoes, chopped small. Now!

The little stove was slow, and there was a lot of soup in the kettle. They still had to stir it occasionally to keep the vegetables from settling to the bottom and burning, but the spaghetti would have been a lot worse. But that was not their worry. Tomorrow night the boys would have their turn at cooking, and it would probably be spaghetti.

Mr. Montgomery Wentworth was a very good nature photographer. When he made a nature documentary, everything had to be just right. He took pictures of whatever the assignment was about, but he also took pictures of other things around about, so that the finished film was almost like a story.

He had followed the tiny stream of water, which was the head of the river, up the hill to a spot where it seemed to flow out of the ground, and then he climbed still farther.

Back in the camp, the soup on the tiny stove had heated thoroughly, so the girls turned the stove burner down to 'simmer' and followed him to the top of the hill, slipping and skidding and climbing over fallen logs.

Suddenly he stopped and lowered himself to his knees. He aimed the camera at a pile of brown leaves beside a rotten log. The girls stopped like frozen statues and stared in the direction the camera was pointing. At first, they saw nothing; just an old log with dead leaves around it.

Then, on the gray-brown log, a gray-brown spider crouched motionless as a stick. It was just a common spider, the exact color of the log, with two legs doubled under it, making it look like it was sitting.

Then there came a small beetle hurrying along from nowhere, running on its tiny black legs. The unwary beetle came close to the spider without slowing down.

In a split instant, the beetle was scooped into the air on a sticky strand and wrapped in a length of silk that the spider had pulled up, seemingly, out of nowhere.

The spider left the beetle hanging on its web and went again to wait on the log. A blue-black wasp stopped on the log, flicking its wings nervously. The spider flung its silk web at the wasp, but the wasp had been on guard and it flew away. The spider sat back down. Was the show over?

The photographer remained on his knees, so the girls did not move. A gray-brown lizard was edging up the side of the log. One tiny, long-toed foot after the other, and it came, easing carefully toward the waiting spider. The girls tried not to breathe. Another step and then another as the lizard came closer. The shiny pinhead eyes of the lizard glistened, unblinkingly. One more step, then a sudden movement and the spider was gone. It happened in an instant. The lizard swallowed several times until the spider was completely past its throat, and then it proceeded toward the silk-wrapped beetle. Another flick of the tongue and the beetle was gone, silk threads and all.

The lizard slowly lowered its body to the log and allowed its eyes to droop, relaxing in the last warm rays of the late afternoon sun. It had a full stomach, and it had been a good day for the lizard.

When the photographer stood up, it was a signal that the girls could again make noise.

"That was a lucky lizard, huh, Dad?" Darla commented.

"Yes," came the answer, "but before tomorrow, the lizard may become lunch for a snake or a coyote."

"Then the coyote would be the lucky one," decided Sally.

"Yes, unless it was caught by a bear or a mountain lion."

"Does it ever end? What happens to the bear or lion?"

"Wolves, vultures, and even the little black beetle are what happens to the coyote or the bear. That's the way it works until humans get into the act. They often change things a lot."

They trudged up the ridge of the mountain. It was very difficult to tell where the exact top of it was.

"You know what, Dad? If we had a really long garden hose and could squirt water up in the air, we could stand here and just watch which way it goes."

"Good idea, except that we don't have a hose. We think the rain clouds may take care of that little problem for us."

"But how will we know where to be when it starts to rain?"

"We'll do some looking around, and we'll film several places. One of them will likely be right. See this flat rock? It slopes both ways.

Look at the little bush growing up out of the crevasse in the rock. Which way do you think the bush leans?"

"West, I think. Is that way west?"

"Yes, that way is west. We'll see what happens when it rains."

Darla was looking around. "Dad, where is that pointed mountain you took a picture of? I haven't seen it since we got here."

"Possibly there are too many trees around us for you to see."

"I guess so, but still...."

At that moment, a voice came from the campsite. "Hey, Dad?"

"Yes, son?" Dad called back.

"Danny and I are going hunting with the bows. Is that all right?"

"No, it isn't. You wait right there until I come down."

"But it'll be too dark by then," complained Dennis.

"I said wait."

The afternoon sun sent its slanting rays through the trees. A breeze was blowing up from the valley, bringing moist, chilly air.

"I'm hungry," complained Darla. "I'll bet that soup is just right. I want to eat."

"Me, too," Sally agreed. "I hope a raccoon doesn't steal the crackers, like last time."

Darla turned to her father to tell him they were going back to camp, but she said nothing. The photographer was kneeling with his camera pointed toward a cedar tree. Inside the dark green, shadowy limbs was a bird nest. Little round heads with wide open mouths were waving unsteadily toward their mother. The mother bird held a fat caterpillar in her mouth.

The baby bird nearest to the mother bird leaned toward her and got the worm into its mouth. But then, in an instant, the mother bird pulled the worm from the baby's mouth and poked it into the mouth of another bird. In an instant, the worm was gone and the second bird opened its mouth for more.

The girls were quiet until the camera stopped running.

"That hateful old mama bird! Did you see that? She likes one of her babies better than the other one. She pulled the food right up out of the mouth of one and put it in another's mouth."

"Yeah, let's find a worm to give to that first little bird."

"It wouldn't help," Dad told them. "The bird wouldn't be able to swallow it."

"Why? Is it sick?"

"No, it's full. The mother bird knew he was full, because he couldn't swallow the worm, so she gave it to another bird. That way, when she and her mate come in with food, they don't have to remember who has eaten last. They poke the food into the first mouth they see and wait for it to go down." Dad was folding his tripod and putting his camera back into its case.

"Really, Dad? Is that true about the worm?"

"Sure is. And speaking of being full, let's go look in on our dinner. I hope you girls have it just about ready and that it tastes as good as it smells."

They slipped and slid down from the ridge of the mountain to the camp. The campsite was quiet, and the boys were nowhere in sight. Sally stirred the kettle of soup. The aroma of meat and vegetables was almost impossible to resist. "Let's eat now. The boys can eat when they come back."

"Come back from where?" asked Dad.

"I don't know, but they're gone."

"DENNIS? DANNY?" called Dad.

The echo came back. "'ennis? 'anny?" but there was no answer from the boys.

"DENNIS, ANSWER ME!" demanded their dad in his 'this is serious business' voice. Still no answer.

Sally stopped stirring the soup, and Darla looked at the wall inside the helicopter. "They took their bows and arrows, Dad. They're gone."

"Hmmmm," thought Dad, biting his lip and stroking his chin. He looked at the ground for footprints and scuffed leaves.

"They went this way," he told the girls as he started down the steep hill. "Come on and go with me. We have to stay together."

Sally reluctantly put the lid back on the steamy soup kettle and turned down the fire as low as it would go, and she followed Darla as they slipped, slid and scooted through the dry leaves down the hill.

The trail stopped at a rock ledge, and there at their feet was the archery bows and quiver of arrows. They were here, all right.

Dad leaned over the ledge. "I see footprints down there. They went in the cave. Let's go on down, girls, and you'll have to wait for me right here at the mouth of the cave. Now, don't you go away."

From deep inside the cave came the faint echo, "...AD?"

"DENNIS?"

"...AD?"

Then, "In here, Dad!" came a clearer voice.

"Danny?"

"Dad?"

The sounds of voices came from far inside the cave. Dad's voice was now becoming fainter. The girls looked at each other and said nothing.

A flutter of bats came out of the cave, causing the girls to duck. The bats flew down into the dark valley, and night birds called from the trees around them. Many frogs chirruped in the pools made by the stream. But no more sounds came from inside the cave.

A screech owl trilled his blood-tingling call and was answered by another owl in a nearby tree.

"I'm scared," confided Sally.

"Me, too. Maybe we should go help them. Dad said not to, but...."

Sally shook her head. "I'm scared to go in there, too. I wish we had a light."

"Or a fire. Guess what! I have matches in my pocket. But it's really too windy for a fire."

"Just a little one? Don't you think...?"

"Well, here, just inside the cave mouth might be all right. It's out of the wind, and there are no dead leaves close by. Can you see well enough to find some little sticks?"

"Dead leaves would start a fire quicker."

"I know, but they would blow all over the place and maybe catch the woods on fire."

In the deepening darkness, the girls heaped a small pile of twigs together and lit a match. They sat close to the fire for warmth and also because they had heard that wild animals were afraid of fire. There were still no sounds from within the cave. There were, however, some sounds in the leaves nearby them. Fright bumps arose on their arms as they huddled closer together.

"I see it!" whispered Darla.

"What is it?" Sally answered.

"I don't know, but it isn't very dangerous. See how close together its eyes are?" Darla pointed to the two shiny dots in the darkness.

"How can you tell from that? Snakes' eyes are close together, and they don't have to be very big to be dangerous."

"Yeah, but remember snakes are cold-blooded, and they can't move around so good after the sun goes down and the wind gets cold. It's probably a rabbit or a raccoon, but I wish you hadn't said what you did about snakes." Darla picked up a twig and tossed it toward the two shiny dots. The dots disappeared and hippity hop sounds came from the darkness as the rabbit scurried down the hill.

"EEEEKK!" yelled Darla, jumping up.

"What is it?"

"Oh, just a toad, but he startled me," Darla said as she tossed the toad away. "He must have been looking for a place to get warm."

Then the voices came dimly from within the cave. The girls stared into the blackness of the cave's mouth, and finally two pinpoints of light appeared. Dad's headlamp and the lantern on his belt bobbed as he walked along.

Then came Dennis, being helped to walk along. Dad was on one side and Danny was on the other. He was dripping wet, with his clothes plastered to his body. Danny's shirt was wet, and he carried it over his arm.

"What happened?" demanded Darla.

"We'll tell you later. Right now, we have to get back up that hill in the dark."

Dad took the small rope off his belt and tied one end of it to the belt of Darla's jeans. He threaded the other end through Sally's belt and tied a knot.

"I'm not going to lose any more people tonight," he said as he tied the other end to Danny's belt.

"Now we're going up the hill, and we'll be crawling slowly because of Dennis' ankle, but we'll all get there. Either we will all get there or none of us will." Somehow the last statement was not very comforting.

The steep hill that was so easy to slide down a short time ago now seemed like a solid wall extending upward.

"One step after another and keep moving," Dad instructed. "Danny, you first. With all the noise we make, nothing should come close to us. Let's go."

They went to their hands and knees and shuffled along in the dark, crawling through the dead leaves and over fallen tree trunks. After what seemed to be forever, they reached the campsite.

The kettle of soup had simmered until it was steaming, thick and tasty.

"Darla, where did you put the crackers?"

"Right there by the stove."

"Really? I hope the raccoons liked them."

"Again? Oh, boy! Well, we've got more. I'll get them out of the chopper."

In the light of the lantern, they ladled soup into deep bowls and crumbled crispy crackers into it. They set water on the stove to heat for their bedtime hot chocolate, and fortunately, the marshmallows had not been set out where the animals could get them.

"Oh," remembered Danny. "We left our bows down at the cave."

"They'll keep," Dad said. "Why did you go hunting when I told you not to?"

After a moment of silence, Danny tried to explain, "We weren't really hunting. We just took our bows along as we walked down the hill to see if we could see that pointed mountain."

"But we didn't get out of sight of the camp," justified Dennis.

Dad nodded, "Perhaps not, but then you decided to go inside the cave."

"Yeah," Danny admitted. "But we saw the bats come out of there, and we wanted to see what bats look like when they hang down from the ceiling asleep."

"And instead of that, you found the bottomless pool."

"Bottomless?" came Sally's frightened voice.

"Do you mean that, Dad?" Darla asked.

"Oh, there's a bottom somewhere down there, but Dennis sure didn't find it when he fell in. Then he came up the first time to discover the sides were too slippery to hold to and, of course, these two cave explorers had no light with them. The water was so far down that Danny couldn't reach down to him without falling in. By the time Dennis came up again, Danny had his shirt off and Dennis grabbed a sleeve. Good thinking, Danny, but it shouldn't have happened at all."

The boys were silent, and Dad continued.

"Dennis couldn't have stood the cold water much longer and Danny couldn't leave him because there was nothing to tie the shirt to, to hold him up while Danny went for help. They were stuck there, and they were so far back in the cave we couldn't hear them call for help until we were at the mouth of the cave."

"Sorry, Dad."

"Did you see it?" Sally asked.

"See what?"

"The pointed hill?"

"No, we didn't. I guess we lost it."

"You're silly. How could anyone lose a hill?"

"Either we lost it or someone stole it. Anyway, it's gone."

The breeze blowing up the mountainside became a strong wind and whistled through the limbs of the trees. The campfire they had built on a flat rock was crackling and warm, and they huddled closer. Dennis still shivered inside the thick blanket Dad had wrapped around him.

Dad poured mugs of hot chocolate, and while they sipped, he told them, "It's time for our evening devotion. We'll do it like we always do. Each of you think of a Bible verse you remember and explain to us why you chose that one. Who's first?"

There was a pause. "I guess I'm first," Dennis offered. "Mine is 'Children, obey your parents that your days may be long'. I just about put an end to mine because I didn't obey."

Danny followed his brother. "Mine is 'I will give you rest'. I was getting very tired of trying to stay on that slippery ledge, holding to one shirt sleeve while he held to the other. I was getting cold, too. I'm glad to have a rest."

Dad nodded his head. "Fine. Now girls?"

"I'm still thinking. Oh, I've got it now. 'I will lift up my eyes unto the hills from where comes my help.' We came down the hill to pull Dennis out."

"All right. Now Sally."

"'Thou preparest a table before me.' I'm ready to eat, and I think I've been hungry for hours. Maybe years."

"Very good. Mine is, 'Make straight paths for your feet.' God does not expect us to go where we might fall. We must watch where we are going and make sure He is leading us. Now, who is ready for that delicious-smelling soup?"

It was inky dark on the mountain when they had finished eating, and they went straight to bed. Dennis was glad for the warmth of the tent, and everyone else was tired. The wind rocked the helicopter gently back and forth even though it was tied down securely to the rock. The coverall-clad girls swayed in their hammock while the small forest animals were left to sniff up the smell of the stew and taste the foam plastic mugs.

The first rays of the sun hit the mountaintops very early. Each bird on the entire mountain peak seemed to be trying to sing louder than its neighbor. Squirrels chattered as the slithering snakes seemed to invade their territory.

The smell of bacon wafted its tantalizing aroma around the doors and into the tent and the chopper, awakening four sleepyheads.

Dad always made breakfast. His campfire biscuits were heavy and thick, perfect for stuffing with bacon or sausage. Or they could be stuffed with scrambled eggs. Then, for dessert, they were stuffed with butter and jam. When everyone was stuffed with biscuits, it would be time for the day to begin.

The morning light was perfect for shooting film. A box turtle with dew drops on his back came by, and he became the star of his own movie as he climbed upon a rock, his tummy shell scraping the surface of the rock. He waddled to the edge of the rock, flipping to his back as he fell to the ground. He flailed his feet in the air and levered his body right-side-up again. Then he shuffled off to wherever turtles shuffle off to.

A butterfly did its exercises on a flower, lifting his wings, then flattening them. It was hard to believe this beautiful butterfly was really just a grownup worm. How did all of these marvelous changes come about?

The only sounds on the mountaintop were the footsteps and voices and the sounds of the insects and animals. Then a resounding "BANG" erupted, echoing through the valley and bouncing off several mountains.

The Wentworths and Sally all stopped instantly and turned toward the explosion, but with all the echoes, it was hard to tell exactly where the sound came from.

"What was that noise, Dad? A gunshot?"

"It sounded more like dynamite, but who would be blasting out here and why? There are no towns close by and no roads are being built. I don't know why anyone would be blasting."

"I thought it came from that flat-topped mountain over there, but I'm not sure."

"Too many echoes."

"Let's fly around and see if we can see something, huh, Dad?"

"No," the photographer told them. "I'll be busy for a while. If it happens again, perhaps we can do a little investigating."

Mr. Wentworth carefully carried a bucket of water to the flat rock at the top of the ridge. He gently poured the water out on the rock and watched it spread. Sure enough, some went west and down over the hill toward California and the Pacific Ocean. The rest of the water flowed to the east where, if it didn't dry up or soak into the ground, it would finally reach the Arkansas River and be carried to the Mississippi River and on out into the Gulf. This was the perfect place to film this assignment.

He set up his tripod and attached a camera securely to it. That camera would take a continuous movie of the center of the rock when the rain came. He would use another camera for additional shots from other angles. A cloud drifted overhead and the photographer raised his camera to film it. The storm would be moving in soon.

Another cloud, a black one, was approaching, and behind it came a solid bank of blackness. The eastern sky was bright and shiny, but the west was dark from the approaching storm. The film in both cameras was running.

"BANG" came another explosion. Almost as a reflex action, the photographer aimed his camera toward the noise just as a pinhead-sized shape arose up out of the trees. Still being filmed, the pinhead became a marble, then a baseball. Finally, it became a small bubble helicopter, buzzing its way through the mountain valley. The photographer adjusted the zoom lens to bring the aircraft closer.

The small chopper did not pause but flew determinedly down the valley, staying lower than the mountaintops.

"Boy, Dad! What was that?"

"I don't know, Danny, but I'll be willing to bet the people in the chopper don't know we're up here."

"Or taking their picture, huh, Dad?"

The dark mountain of clouds was closer now, and fiery lightning bolts zig-zagged out of their blackness. The hand-held camera recorded all of their flaming strikes at the forested mountains.

One bolt of lightning struck a tree on the opposite hill, causing a fire to blaze up. Fanned by the wind, the dry leaves burned quickly, and the fire raced toward the top of the hill as it acted in its own movie. For a while, the fire was the star of the film, but then the raindrops started to fall.

The humans on the mountain ran for their boots and slickers, but the camera action did not stop. Large drops splattered wetly on the dry rock, turning it from silver gray to a dull charcoal. The water filled the cracks and dimples of the rock and then began to flow. Some of the water flowed west and some flowed east.

The camera on the tripod recorded the rain that fell on the little bush that grew out of the rock. Rainwater dripped from the pointed leaves of the bush and flowed toward the west on its way to California and the Pacific Ocean. Then the wind blew harder and the bush swayed before it, spraying water drops all over the rock. Now, a lot of the drops fell on the east side of the rock and flowed in the other direction.

"Look Dad! See what a difference the wind makes?"

A rivulet of water ran off the rock and through the dead leaves. It formed a puddle in a hollow rock, and then the puddle overflowed. It joined another rivulet of water and flowed faster, forming the beginning of the little mountain stream.

The photographer filmed the eastward stream and then climbed back up the hill again. He would continue with that stream later, but he needed to get some shots of the westward stream while it was still raining.

The triplets and Sally had climbed into the helicopter out of the rain. It was coming down harder now and put out the fire caused by the lightning. The large drops of water beat against the top and sides of the helicopter and streamed over the windows. Fog from their breath coated the inside of the windows, and they drew pictures in the condensed vapor. Still, the lightning blazed and thunder crackled and echoed from mountaintop to mountaintop.

"Look, the lightning fire has drowned out."

"It sure has."

"What do you think happened to that pointed mountain?"

"I don't know. Can I see those picture again?"

"See, we're right here. There's the flat-topped mountain in the picture, and the pointed one is right beside it."

"What's making that point?"

"It looks like a great big old rock, doesn't it?"

"Now look out there. The pointed rock is just to the left of the flat-topped one."

"No, it isn't."

"Then where did it go?"

"Maybe it washed away?"

"It couldn't have. It has that big rock on top of it, remember?"

"Besides, these pictures were made only a few months ago, and it wouldn't have been able to wash away in that length of time."

"Then where is it?"

"I don't know."

"The whole thing is weird."

"Worse than that. It's spooky."

Then Mr. Wentworth came back with the camera. "That's all the pictures we need until after the storm. We should have some very good shots. For once, the weatherman made a perfect prediction."

The chopper was really steamy now with so many people breathing in it.

"We should have gone down to the cave where we would have a lot more room."

"No, no! Not me!" announced Sally.

"Why not?"

"It's too scary! It almost got Dennis."

"Now wait a minute," Dad cut in. "There's nothing wrong with the cave. Dennis wouldn't have fallen in if he had taken proper precaution. A lot of caves have water in them, so he should not have gone charging into it without a light. A lot of these mountains have large, hollow places in them, and very few of them are perfectly dry caves. Strange shapes were created while the mountain range was formed."

They were silent for a few minutes.

Dad continued. "If the storm lasts a long time, we'll make our evening camp in the cave. Things in nature can be good or bad, depending on how they're used, and the cave would be a very good place to camp if we didn't have the tent and the chopper."

It was granola bars for lunch because the rain did not stop. By early afternoon, they had slogged down to the cave. The boys stood in the mouth of the cave and shot three rabbits with their arrows. Darla and Sally played tic-tac-toe in the dust of the cave floor while the photographer thumbed through a magazine.

"When the storm stops tomorrow, we'll go to the valley and trace this little stream on down the valley for a little way," Dad told them.

"But what if the storm never stops?"

"Then we'll have a lot of rabbits to eat and play a lot of tic-tac-toe games."

"Aw, Dad!"

By dinnertime, there were two more rabbits to be skinned, and the five of them were strung up on green sticks over a crackling fire in the mouth of the cave. The smell of the roasting meat was almost maddeningly delicious. No spaghetti tonight!

There was hot chocolate at bedtime and more memory verses from the Bible.

"'In my father's house are many mansions. I go to prepare a place for you.' I'm anxious to know what that place is going to look like," offered Darla.

"'And she brought forth her first born Son.' That's when Jesus was born so we could have Christmas. I love Christmas!"

"Let me see. 'I do set my bow in the cloud.' That's what God told Noah when He promised He would not destroy the world with water again. I want to see a rainbow the first thing tomorrow, because that will mean the rain has stopped."

"I have one. 'The hairs of your head are all numbered.' I'm glad someone knows that much about me, especially when my hair is full of tangles."

"This is mine. 'Commit your ways unto the Lord and He will direct your path.' We don't have to worry about which is the right way to go. All we have to do is follow Jesus, and we will go the right way. Now look out there, and you will see that the rain has stopped. We can climb the hill and sleep in our own beds."

Morning came and the sun was again shining warm against the tent and the helicopter, and the smell of bacon was again in the air. The fat biscuits lured the sleepyheads out of their beds and to the campfire. Dad's coffee perked merrily on its own little stove.

When the biscuits stuffed with bacon had been stuffed into mouths, Dad told them, "We'll untie the chopper so we can follow the stream to the valley. We'll leave the tent and the gear up here because we'll probably want to stay here another night."

The tie-downs were loosed from the helicopter and the long blades were put in motion, rotating slowly, then faster. The chopper lifted up and swung off the flat rock at the top of the ridge and began to descend, noisily, toward the valley.

"Keep your eyes on the stream. Here, Darla, try to follow it with the camera, and we'll see what we get."

Darla pointed the camera lens toward the small stream as it fell like liquid silver over a large rock. It splashed into a pool and was hidden within the trees for a space. Then there it was again. It was bigger and bluer now, because another stream had joined it, and the early morning silver of the reflected sky was now the blue of a clear mountain morning. Darla held the camera as steadily as possible considering the movement of the chopper.

It was a long way down to the valley, and by the time the stream reached the bottom, it had grown into a rushing little river. The larger stream of water rushing through the valley caught up the mountain stream and whisked it away. Some of the drops of water in the valley were tumbling along toward the Pacific Ocean only because the wind on the ridge had not blown the bush to the east. Amazing!

"Let's look at another stream, Dad."

"Fine, but I want more footage of this steam first."

"Hey, Dad?"

"Yes, Kitten?"

"When we get through there, let's go look at the pointed mountain."

"The one that isn't there? Fine. Now as we go back up the mountain, I want you to keep the camera on the stream all the way. Come over here beside me so you can get a better view. Can you do that?"

"Sure, Dad."

The chopper worked its way up from the valley, following the course of the falling water. Dad held the aircraft as steadily as possible while dodging treetops and allowing for wind shifts.

Back at the campsite and now finished with the pictures of the stream, they decided to fly out and around the pointed mountain before coming in close to it. Perhaps they could determine why it was no longer pointed. The chopper swung off the large rock once more and flew out over the valley. Four noses were pressed against the window glass as they came closer to the mountain that should be there... but wasn't.

As they followed the valley, they saw something that caused them to gasp. Instead of being covered with green leaves and gray-brown tree trunks, the mountain had a huge gash of freshly disturbed earth all the way down one side. The red color of the dirt was like a giant grave on the mountainside. Yesterday's rain had caused streams of red water from the exposed clay to run in streaks on the ground. Instead of the silver and blue of the water, the streams held red-brown liquid, flowing sluggishly. The mountain appeared to have a large, bleeding wound.

"Look what that rainstorm did to the mountain, Dad," Dennis pointed out. "It's washing the dirt into the valley."

"Yuck! Look how it's changing the color of the little river."

"The storm didn't do that, boys."

"Then what did?"

"I don't know yet. We'll circle on around and see what else there is to see."

The helicopter swung away from the treetops and followed the side of the strange mountain. Ah, there was another muddy spot on the other side of the mountain, and it was even bigger than the first one. The stream of mud flowing downhill was striped with red from the clay and chocolate brown from the mountain topsoil.

"Dad, that mountain is coming apart. See, there's more dirt over there." Danny pointed to the third bare spot. Beside it was a trail of broken trees and gouged out places. At the bottom of the hill, laying there in the mountain valley, was the huge, gray, pointed stone from the top of the hill. It had slid into the valley, toppling trees as it slid. The water had backed up against the gray rock, making a small, muddy lake. Large cracks and fissures were visible. When the large rock protected the top of the mountain, the cracks and fissures were hidden caves and caverns, honeycombing the mountain. The sliding of the mammoth rock had torn into their walls.

"Hmmmm," was Dad's only comment as he circled and made another pass at the strange holes.

"Maybe a meteor hit the mountain?"

"Or a shooting star?"

"Could someone be mining something out of this hill?"

"Cutting timber too closely, maybe?"

"Landslide from all the rain?"

"Lightning?"

"What are you thinking, Dad?"

"Yeah, Dad, what do you think it is?"

"He doesn't know, either."

"Hey, why are we going away? I wanted to see some more."

"I'll bet he's going back to camp."

"Dad...?"

The helicopter circled the holes in the mountain and flew back down into the valley, but when they reached the mountain stream, they did not follow it up the hill again. The chopper proceeded on down the valley.

"See, we're not going to camp."

"Then where?"

Finally Dad answered. "We're low on fuel," he explained.

"Then can we come back here?"

"Can we land on that other mountain?"

"On one of those muddy spots?"

"No, we'd get stuck."

"I meant beside it."

"Of course, that's what he's going to do, or we wouldn't need to get more gas."

The helicopter set down on the outskirts of the small town of Granite, near a truck stop.

"I'm hungry, Dad."

"Me, too."

"There's a burger place."

"Huh, Dad?"

"He sees it. I'll bet he's hungry, too."

They were busily munching thick, juicy burgers when a small bubble chopper swooped low over the Wentworth helicopter and circled out and around it before working its way out into the valley.

A tiny bubble helicopter threaded its way among the mountains like a huge bumble bee searching for just the right flower.

"Told ya there wasn't nothin' to worry about," the well-rounded, whiskered chopper pilot told his skinny passenger.

"I know that, Lefty, but you tell me lots of things, and most of them need checkin' out before bein' believed. Seems like you could have been right this time," Elmer agreed. "All the same, it was worth takin' the time to check. That big chopper could have been nosy law men 'stead of a passel of kids on a campout."

"Told ya it was jist campers. Told Bart, too. Next time ya could both be listenin', and we'd save the time of buzzin' up and down this valley. Told ya there wasn't nothin' but crows and mountain rattlers out there, and you worryin' is keepin' us from work."

After a moment, Elmer nodded. "I'm hopin' that's all that's out there, but I found out long time ago that there wasn't never a time I was sorry I was careful." The whirling propeller followed the valleys, being careful not to rise above the tops of the mountains.

"When we drag the last load up here and move on, it'll be none too soon for me. I get the heebie-jeebies bein' in one place so long like this," Lefty admitted.

The silver-blue river below them sparkled with its small waterfalls, and it rested peacefully in its pools. A troop of Boy Scouts had set up their camouflage tents beside one of the small lakes. The smoke of their cooking fire spiraled upward like a silver feather, moving softly in the breeze.

Finally, Elmer responded to Lefty's statement. "You jist go ahead and have all the heebie-jeebies you want or anything else, but we're goin' to finish what we started. Bein' careful all the time, that's the answer to bein' safe."

The Plexiglas bubble of the aircraft paused, hovering in the valley, and then it entered a secluded cove between two mountains, settling gently on a grass-covered ledge.

A man in army fatigue green pants and shirt came toward them as the chopped blade began to slow to a stop.

"Hello, Bart," Lefty greeted him.

"Shore took your time gettin' here, didn't ya? Got a good reason why you was so long?" demanded Bart.

Lefty snorted, "Yeah! Jist ask old Elmer about that. Had me buzzin' up and down every fork of this valley and checkin' out the towns. He had me buzzin' all the way in to Granite."

"To Granite! How come?" The question was directed at Elmer.

Lefty answered for him. "I'll tell you how come. He fancied a chopper full of campers was spyin' on us."

Bart's attitude changed from anger to concern. "What did you find out?"

Lefty sneered again, "The whole passel of them was down at Granite, benched up in a hamburger joint, feedin' their faces."

Bart nodded, relieved. "You did right to check on them. Lots of times, them nature people turn out to be the nosiest kind."

"Nature people? Shucks, they didn't even cook outside. How can they be nature people and go into a town for grub? There they was, all lined up to that bar like pigs to a trough. What I always say...."

"Never mind," butted in Bart. "We already heard all you got to say. You got the cargo?"

"Sure enough have," answered Elmer, unlocking the compartment behind the pilot's seat.

By the time the containers were setting on the ground, Bart had arrived with the steel-runnered sled. Sideboards had been made onto the sled so the five gallon cans could be stacked on it.

"Lefty, put on them gloves like I told you a hundred times. Now all them cans you touched got to be wiped off."

"Aw, nobody ain't goin' to see them cans once we get 'em took care of, and they sure ain't goin' to be lookin' for no fingerprints. Besides, how come you to get so bossy? Them ain't even your fingerprints. They're mine."

"Yeah, and us partnerin' up with you like we had to, it'd be no time at all till your fingerprints was linked up with me."

Lefty looked quickly at Bart. "Hey, you gettin' the heebie-jeebies, too? Then let's get on out of here."

"Nope, we'll stick to the plan. Switchin' around and doin' things without proper thought, that'd be the way to really mess up and call attention to yourself. No, we ain't goin' to move on right now."

Lefty sighed and began to wipe the fingerprints off the cans, and then he put on the gloves, as instructed. Elmer helped Bart pull the loaded sled toward a hole in the mountain. Three sled loads were stowed away.

"Better put some gas in that thing before you make another trip. Goin' down to Granite like you done likely made you run low."

"Sure did and it took up a lot of time, too," Lefty complained. "We're goin' to be late on that next run."

"Hey, are you about through belly-achin' about that side trip? You know you can quit this operation any time you want to."

"Then where'd you be for a pilot that knows mountains like I do? No, I ain't goin' to quit and you can't make me. Another thing, I'm tired of bein' treated like poor relation."

"Jist be glad we put up with you at all. We'd manage for a pilot if you was to quit."

"Well, I ain't gonna and you can't make me."

"I guess not, but they's times I'd like to."

Lefty grinned at them. "But I already know too much, don't I?"

Lefty added fuel to the tank of the aircraft from a storage can inside the cave and climbed into the pilot's seat. Tall Elmer doubled his lanky frame and sat down in the cramped seat beside him. The propeller began to rotate, and the bubble lifted up from the grassy ledge and set off down the valley, flying just above the treetops.

Lefty was still not through discussing his value to the trio. "Another reason for why you ain't gonna push me out of this operation. Neither one of you long lanky lizards can come up with the money for a chopper like mine, even if you was to be able to fly it. They ain't many pilots who can fly like me, down here amongst the bird nests and squirrel tails."

Elmer made no reply. Lefty was an excellent pilot for these ridiculous little egg beaters. A big chopper like the one the campers had would be quicker, but this little bubble was a lot safer for them. Lefty could almost hide this little thing in a bird nest if he had to, and there was always the chance that hiding would be necessary.

Darla and Sally each ate a hamburger and halfed another one between them. It would have been hard to count just how many burgers the boys ate. They bought canned wieners and chili for dinner back at the campsite and headed toward the mountains. The little tent tied down to the rock looked like a matchbox toy from high in the air.

"Hey, Dad, you're passing by the camp."

"Yeah, where are you going, Dad?"

"He's going over to the funny mountain."

"Are you, Dad?"

"Of course he is. See it just ahead?"

"What are you looking for, Dad?"

"I'll bet he's wondering what made all those dirt patches."

"Are you, Dad?"

"I know what it is, Dad. Someone is hauling away dirt to fill up a hole somewhere."

"Well, they're making another hole right here."

"No, they're not hauling dirt. There aren't any roads to be driving on."

"They could fly it out with a chopper."

"Yeah, but that'd cost too much."

"Right, because wherever they took it, they could get dirt a lot closer than this. This place isn't close to anything."

"It's close to us."

"You know what I mean."

"Then what made the holes?"

By now they had reached the damaged mountain. Dad circled the top of the mountains above the area and then began to descend into the valley. A grassy ledge below them was green and inviting. It was almost out of sight down between the two big mountains.

"Danny?"

"Yeah, Dad?"

"We're going to land and step out of the chopper. You are going to keep out of sight inside the chopper and keep a camera on us all the time. None of the rest of you are going to say anything except how pretty everything is up here. Understand?"

"Hey, we're going to be spies!"

"And, Danny," Dad continued. "Keep the door open. We might want to leave here in a hurry."

"I will, Dad."

The helicopter settled gently onto the small, grassy meadow. "Now, kids, you stay on the outside of the ledge and don't go near the mountain, no matter what you see me do."

Darla and Sally went to the edge of the stone ledge and looked over. A pink flower grew out of the rocks just out of reach. Sally stretched out on her stomach and Darla held onto her feet to keep her from slipping over while she picked it.

Dennis walked with Dad. "Look, Dad," he called. "Ripe berries! What kind are these?"

Dad came closer to him. "Strawberries, son. I'll get something to pick them in." Then, in a low whisper, he said, "Dennis, don't move or say anything. Wait right here for me to be back."

Dennis waited, wanting to look around but forcing himself not to do it.

At the helicopter, Dad reached for a used foam coffee cup to use as a container for the berries and whispered, "Danny, get the Polaroid camera and aim at the mountain, but shoot through the peep hole. DO NOT BE SEEN!"

Dad left, and Danny aimed the camera toward the dark face of the mountain and at the even darker hole in the side of it. He clicked and then waited for the print. He clicked again and thought he saw movement at the cave door. How many pictures should he take? Dad hadn't said, so he took another one. This time he knew he saw movement. Then Dad said, loudly... too loudly, actually, "That's all the berries. Let's go. Come on, girls."

"But Dad..." Dennis objected, playing along with the game.

"Time to go," insisted Dad.

Dennis followed along. The girls ran to Dad, showing him the flower. "See, it came up with its roots. Can we take it home and plant it?"

"Now, girls, you know you're not to pull up the native plants. Why did you do that?" He was still speaking loudly and could be clearly heard from some distance away.

"Sorry, Dad," Darla apologized. "I won't do it anymore. But can we have this one?"

"I suppose so, now that you've already pulled it up." In a low whisper, he said to the three of them, "Get in the chopper. Fast!"

"I'll race you girls," Dennis yelled and the girls took out after him. They were breathless as they climbed into the helicopter. Dad came along behind, walking fast and carrying the cup of berries. He yelled, "Dennis, don't you dare start that engine!"

In an instant the sound of the engine echoed from the ledge and bounced off the mountain across the valley.

"DENNIS! STOP THAT!" Dad began to run and he jumped into the helicopter and slammed the door. The propeller was rotating rapidly, and the engine was firing loudly. Dad took the controls and the machine lifted off the ledge. No one said anything until they were well out into the valley.

"You kids did a good job," Dad complimented. "Dennis, you got that engine going so well that I had a good reason to pretend to hurry. Danny, did you get pictures?"

"Sure did, Dad, but I can't make out the shape in the cave door."

"Cave?" Sally asked. "Was there a cave back there?"

"Sure was. Something was in it, too."

"What? A bear?"

"I don't know, but here are the pictures."

"Where are those berries?"

"Right here."

"Is that all you got?"

"Yeah, because Dad made me leave the rest."

"I want one."

"Dad, it looks like a person in the cave door. Or maybe it's a bear standing on its hind legs. No, it's too skinny to be a bear."

"Why would a person be all the way out here?"

"How did he get here? Fly?"

"I want another berry."

"Dad, do you want a berry? Open your mouth. Oops, Dad, I fed you a bug."

"Did you really feed Dad a bug?"

"No, she didn't. I was watching."

"What was in the cave?"

"I don't know. He isn't wearing a name tag."

The helicopter was now following the stream up the long mountain to the campsite.

"Is there another berry?" Sally asked.

"Only one," Darla answered. "We'll divide it."

"We don't have a knife."

"That's alright. Here, you bite off half. Don't bite my finger."

"Then let me hold it."

"No, then you would eat it all."

"I see something else, Dad. It looks like there are strange marks on the ground."

"Footprints?"

"No, streaks. Like something heavy was being dragged around."

"I know what it is, Dad. It's sled runners."

"Aw, how could a sled get up here in the mountains?"

"All the same, that's what it looks like."

"Here, let me see."

"Then wipe the juice off your fingers and don't get my picture messy."

"Your picture?"

"Well, I took it."

"Hey, Dad, it sure does look like sled tracks. What would make a mark like that?"

"Yeah, Dad, what?"

"He doesn't know. He hasn't even seen the picture."

The helicopter settled onto the flat rock and Dad reached for the Polaroid shots Danny had taken of the cave opening. There was an object (human?) at the mouth of the cave, but the light was not bright enough and the camera had not been close enough for the picture to be clear. What could it be? And there's that tiny dot of light like a reflection off something shiny. What was that?

"Gather around and listen, kids. We're going to sleep somewhere else tonight."

"Where?"

"I'll show you. There's a cave near here. I found it when I was looking for a place to shoot. There is also a beautiful valley. We'll check out the valley first. It may be hard to get the chopper down by the cave. The valley will be easier."

"Why?"

"Is somebody after us?"

"But we didn't do anything."

"But they don't know we didn't do anything."

"Who is 'they'?"

"I'll go untie the tent. Come on, Danny."

Dad stopped them. "No, don't go get the tent. I want to see what happens if we leave it. You boys load up the stove but leave those cans and everything we don't have to have to spend the night. Kitten, bring the tripod and come with me. Sally, you get that small waterproof tarpaulin and come along."

With great care, the photographer set up the camera. He focused it on the tent with a time-lapse setting so it would take a picture every three minutes. Then he attached the little sound-sensitive clock. Now, when a loud noise of any kind triggered the clock, the camera would film continuously instead of time-lapse. He covered the camera and its tripod with the camouflage tarp except for the small lens opening.

"Why, Dad, I can't even tell what that is, and I know it's there!"

Back on the rock, the boys had loaded the small stove and its large cooking kettle along with other things they would need for an overnight camp. They climbed aboard, and they were ready. Dad put fresh batteries in the extra flashlight and put it in the tent, setting it up on its end, like a candle, to shine on the ceiling of the tent. Then they were off.

Up, out and over the ridge they climbed. They were so high that fluffy clouds were beside and below them. Down they settled into the valley on the other side of the ridge. A grassy meadow stretched out invitingly as the chopper touched down.

A mother deer watched them for a second, then flipped her furry tail up, showing the white fluffy underside. The fawn saw her signal and was instantly at her side. Two other does with fawns leaped into the meadow, and the six of them were gone in a flash, disappearing into the low bushes.

"That would have made a good picture," Sally commented.

"Maybe they'll come back," offered Darla.

Everyone jumped out onto the grassy ground.

"Dad, if someone was trying to catch us, wouldn't they see us down here? We need to put on the camouflage cover, don't we?" suggested Danny.

"I'll get it," Dennis offered.

"Wait, Dennis. Dad, if we put on the camouflage cover, will you make the girls heat up dinner?"

Darla shook her head. "No, Dad, it's their turn. We'll put on the cover."

"Aw, Dad."

"Yeah," agreed Sally, "we can do it as well as you. Which side do you want, Darla? I'll climb up on top to pull it over."

There, in the tip top of a pitifully small tree, swaying back and forth, was a fat, full-grown raccoon, peering intently at the camera. His shiny eyes glistened in his black bandit mask. He wriggled the end of his nose, lifting his lips slightly to show tiny pointed teeth. His four delicately-toed paws held to the pencil thin limbs as he clung, motionless, watching the camera.

Then the camera stopped. "That's enough of him," Dad decided. "We'll walk away and let him come down. He must be getting tired."

"Dad, can we get our bows and shoot some rabbits?"

"Not today, Danny. We'd have to build a wood fire to roast them to make them really good, and I don't want to have a fire down there tonight. We can hide our cook stove, but we can't hide the smoke of a bonfire."

"Do you really think someone is after us?"

"He said he didn't know."

"Is it about those dirt patches?"

"I'll bet it is."

"Yeah, someone is stealing the mountain."

"No, they're knocking it over. That big rock rolled down the hill, remember?"

"But there's more to it than that. The mountain isn't as big as it was."

"It's like a balloon that someone let some air out of. And it's shaped different."

"But it must be the same mountain...."

"Well, we didn't take it. Why would they be mad at us?"

"Who is 'they'?"

"I'll bet it was whoever was in that cave."

"Whoever it was got a good look at us, didn't they?"

"Not me!" said Danny smugly. "They didn't see me at all!"

They walked through the woodland to a large pool of water. It was so crystal clear that it seemed to be made out of glass.

"Oh, look at the darling tiny fish. I want to take some home for the fish tank."

"Sorry, Kitten, but they wouldn't live. They have to be left here."

"I see a big snapping turtle."

"I do, too. There's another one."

"Let's catch them. They don't have to be roasted."

"I got one! Watch out!" Darla held the dinner-plate sized turtle by the tail. Everyone jumped away from its snapping jaws.

"Put it on its back, Kitten. Right here!"

The turtle was put down, and Dad got out his long-bladed hunting knife and removed its head. "Two more of these and we'll have turtle soup for breakfast. Or fried turtle for dinner."

"Or both? I see a lot of turtles."

They pulled six turtles from the mud beside the pool. Sally ran back to the campsite for the kettle. By the time she had returned, there was a large pile of juicy turtle meat, glistening white after the skin had been pulled away.

"Boys, take the meat back to camp and start frying it."

"Aw, Dad...."

"Move it! We'll be coming right along."

"But Dad, we shot the rabbits for last night. It's really their turn again."

"Not so," insisted Dad. "We take turns cooking and no cooking was done with the rabbits. They roasted themselves. Now scram."

They took some pictures of the small fish in the pool and then went back to camp. Dennis and Danny were busy with the turtle meat.

"You can turn them this time. I popped some grease on my fingers and it hurts."

"So now you want mine to hurt? I told you to wait till we found the big fork."

"Then we'd never eat because I think the big fork is back up on top of the ridge."

"Hurry up! It's going to burn."

"Well, it's either me or the turtle."

"Let it be you. Turn the turtle. I'm hungry."

"Oh, give me that little fork. I'll do it. Hey, these pieces are done. Hand me the plate."

"Here it is."

"No, get a bigger plate. I have six more pieces to put on it. Now, you can put the next batch in the skillet."

When all the turtle meat was browned and crusty, it was returned to the kettle and two cups of water were added. The lid was put back on and weighed down with a rock. In ten minutes it would be ready to eat.

The delicious smell of the turtle would even make the rocks hungry if they had noses. Chili and wieners were good, but in a race for best, they lost out to fried turtle every time. Everyone ate until they were stuffed and could hold no more and licked their fingers. Then they sat on the soft grass and sipped their evening chocolate.

"I have my Bible verse ready. 'Man shall not live by bread alone.' I think a little turtle meat is nice, too."

"And what else?" asked Dad.

"Spaghetti?"

"Yes, and what else?"

"I know, Dad. It's the rest of the verse. It says, 'Man shall not live by bread alone but every word that Jesus says'. That means that what Jesus says is as important as food."

"Right. Next?"

"Mine is 'I will trust and not be afraid'," said Sally. "But I guess I really am afraid... at least, just a little."

"I have a good one. 'He maketh me to lie down in green pastures.' That is from the psalm that David wrote, and see here? We have the green pasture all around us."

"That's right," Dad said. "But you're not going to lie down on it. You're going to sleep in the chopper tonight."

"With us?" objected Darla.

"Yes, all five of us will sleep in there."

"Aw, Dad...."

"Next?"

"I have it. 'He leadeth me beside the still water.' That's more of the 23rd Psalm, and that's where we caught the turtles... in the still water. Now you, Dad."

Dad nodded. "Mine is 'Consider the lilies of the field. They toil not, neither do they spin, yet Solomon, rich as he was, was not dressed as beautifully as they are'. That means that no matter what we do, we cannot improve on nature and the best thing we can do is not as good as God's smallest miracle."

"Dad?"

"Yes, Dennis?"

"Who has to make the turtle soup for breakfast? It's for tomorrow, but it has to be put on the stove today. So who has to do it?"

"Girls' turn," was Dad's decision.

"Aw, Dad..." Darla groaned.

"Thanks, Dad!" gloated Danny.

Darla stood and looked down her nose at her brothers. "Dad just wanted us to do it because we can do it so much better. Come on, Sally. We've got to go hunting in the supply box for the onion flakes and the dried parsley."

It was getting dark as Lefty steered the bubble of a helicopter up the valley.

"Ain't real fond of dodgin' treetops in the dark," Lefty complained.

"Don't fuss at me. Weren't my fault that highway was swarmin' alive with the law. I'd rather be late than get picked out of the sky with a lawman bullet."

"They wasn't after us. I told ya that. They don't even know about us."

"You don't know that. You know what Bart said about bein' safe."

"Yeah, but him sayin' a thing don't make it true."

"Does this time. Hey, ease up that mountain for a look-see. I think I saw somethin'."

"Then we'll be later than we are."

"I wouldn't worry about that."

"Of course you wouldn't worry. It ain't you tryin' not to hit the bird nests with this eggbeater."

"Shut up and get yourself on up that hill."

The bubble arose and followed the silver-blue stream of water to the ridge of the mountain. The little tent stood on the flat rock with various pieces of equipment laying around.

"See? Campers. They got that tent pitched too close to us to suit me."

"Looks almost deserted."

"Naw, they'll be out looking for mushrooms or wild something-or-others. They'll be back, mark my word."

"But they ain't no threat to us."

"You don't know that. Let's go on, now."

"Thanks. We done wasted twenty minutes, and now it's black dark."

"So now you don't have to hide in the trees no more."

They landed on the ledge, and Bart came to meet them.

"Wasn't my fault we was late," Lefty announced.

"Can the chatter, numbskull. We got us bigger troubles than you bein' late."

"Troubles?"

"Yeah. A big chopper full of flower-sniffers stopped here a few hours ago and looked the place over."

"Did they see you?"

"No, but I'd wager it's the same ones you followed down to Granite. A feller and some half-grown kids."

Elmer nodded. "Same ones. Lookin' for trouble, was they?"

"They didn't say nothin', but them flower sniffers are as much trouble as the law any day, always snoopin' where they got no business. Hurry up and unload. We got some thinkin' to be done. Lefty, you put on them gloves."

"Sure, sure. And maybe I should put a hanky on the sled before I load it."

"Might not be such a bad idea," retorted Elmer.

After three sled loads had been deposited, the cargo was out of sight.

"Now we got to talk," announced Bart.

"Yeah, I'd wager a dollar to a toothpick it's the same people campin' over on the next hill," Elmer decided.

"But there weren't no chopper there."

"Makes no difference. Same folks, all right. They's a lot of space out here. Chance of havin' two bunches of flower sniffers that close together ain't reasonable."

"What'll we do?"

"We got guns...."

"Hate to go that far."

"Wouldn't you hate to get caught?"

"Yeah, but...."

"Lefty, can you find that camp in the dark?"

"I 'speck so. I found my way here in the dark, didn't I?"

"Don't get huffy. I was jist askin'."

Bart scratched his chin. "Elmer, you get that gun, and I'll take this one here. We'll scatter some shot around them to put a scare into them, and then we got to get out. Even if we hit one of them, they ain't got no way to trace it to us."

"We ain't gonna leave here yet, are we? We still got lots of space in that mountain that ain't got nothin' in it."

"And it's got to stay that way. We got to go on. It's the only safe way."

"Bart, you forgettin' about what we got to do with them cans? They still got labels on them, and they'd be traced to us in no time at all."

"Don't worry. I took care of that while I was waitin' on you."

"What do you mean, you took care of them! You ain't no dynamite man?"

"No, but I watched you time and again, and I got it all strung up, ready to blow. We'll fly up to that camp and then come back here and set it off. I hate to leave here so soon, but some things just got to be done. We could have stayed here all summer if them mushroom chompers would have stayed out of the way. They deserve anything they get from our guns."

"You mean you got everything strung up and ready to blow? All by yourself?"

"Said I did."

"But...."

"Now, Elmer, you think you are the only person that can do a job?"

"No offense. We ready now?"

The chopper lifted off the ledge and into the dark valley. The moon was bright on the leaves of the trees and their smooth surfaces glowed a reflection. The tiny stream was made of cut diamonds, sparkling and twisting about as they fell. Higher and higher the bubble climbed toward the tent on the flat rock. Even in the bright moonlight it was plain to see the light from within the tent. The flashlight glowed warmly through the open door.

"Hey, look. They're in there."

"Where at is that big chopper?"

"Gone to Granite, probably. Left the nature kids here to earn their survival badges."

"Now, we ain't goin' to shoot down there at kids, are we?" objected Lefty.

"You ain't shootin' nothin'. You jist tend to the flyin'."

"But you two are gonna to shoot. That'd be the same thing, and them's just kids."

"And kids turn into grownups. Nosy, stupid flower-sniffing grownups. They got to learn a lesson while they're still kids. One that they ain't likely to forget."

"But shootin'?"

"Hush up. Get up a little closer and then turn sideways. I got to get a good aim."

Lefty climbed higher, clenching his teeth. He swung the bubble around, and a staccato of bullets left Bart's gun.

"Now whirl this thing around the other way. Be ready, Elmer."

Elmer's gun was unloaded into the tiny tent. "Some of the bullets hit," he reported. "Look at them holes in the tent showin' the light comin' through." A lot of pinpoints of light were sprinkled over the side of the tent.

"I didn't figure to get in on no shootin'."

"Hush up. We never asked them kids to come sniffin' around, neither. Maybe we jist scair't them."

"And maybe you hit them," muttered Lefty as he turned the bubble toward the quiet, moonlit valley.

Back on the ledge, the men returned to the hole in the rock face of the mountain. Bart looked around at the neatly piled gear.

From the small door in the face of the rock, the cave opened out into a large room extending far back into the mountain. A rock ledge formed the ceiling of the room and another slab of stone made the floor. The layer of dirt between the stone layers had been washed away by the underground stream which ran through it. Centuries of flowing water had created a room almost large enough to be a football field. This was really one big hollowed-out mountain!

Elmer shook his head at Bart and said sadly, "Sure hate to let this one blow. We got so much room left that's gonna be wasted."

Bart agreed. "That little old pile of cans is pitifully small. Could have used this one, maybe, for years. But there ain't no use to be moanin' over it now. What's got to go may as well be on its way. You want to light it?"

"Naw, you go ahead. You done the wirin'."

The men went to the cave entrance. Bart sprinkled a stream of powder over the stretched out cord. "Just addin a little insurance, puttin' the powder on the fuse," he explained to himself.

Elmer made no comment. He sighed as he took one last look at the room before he walked out the door. The bubble aircraft glowed in the moonlight. Lefty was in the pilot's seat and the prop was rotating slowly. Elmer folded himself small enough to climb in beside him. They could see Bart crouch at the cave door and light a match. The tiny blaze caught the fuse, and a spitting, sputtering flame crawled along the cord into the blackness of the mountain.

Then they saw Bart come running across the clearing toward the helicopter and he quickly wedged himself into it. The blades were rotating rapidly now, and the tiny aircraft buzzed its way up the valley to the new site that had been selected some time ago.

The sputtering flame crawled along the fuse until it reached the first knot, then the flame divided, part of it continuing on and another part of it going in another direction.

At the second knot, another division of the flame occurred. At the fifth knot, six flames were burning, and the little helicopter was miles away. The flames were gauged to detonate at a precise time.

The first fuse to blow exploded near a pile of metal containers. The force of the blast blew a hole through the side of the mountain, causing a section of the cave roof to crumble. The second blast made the hole larger. The third one brought down a massive sheet of the stone ledge ceiling and the fourth blast continued the damage.

The slab ceiling crumbled into huge rocks which rolled down into the valley and filled up the cave room. The fifth blast sent up a cloud of dirt and small stones and the sixth one started a landslide that loosened dirt and trees nearby and starting them on their way down to the valley.

The noise and vibration of the first explosion was heard only by the animals on the mountain. All humans were far away.

The second of the blasts had shot flames through the wall, causing hot metal to be flung into the dry leaves. A tiny flame burst up from one of the hot metal can fragments, creating a small fire that flickered and wavered in the night breeze. The flame grew tall but a sudden puff of wind blew it down. The new oxygen the fire received from the breeze strengthened it, and the fire crawled through the layer of leaves like a rabbit through a brushpile, heading toward a dead tree trunk which had fallen many years ago.

Tongues of orange flame licked around the tree trunk, consuming it greedily. The fire was stronger now, and it lifted itself up to the bushes and clumps of grass. Encouraged by the strong wind coming up from the valley, it rapidly climbed the mountain.

Ground-nesting birds scolded the intruding flame before taking to their wings, leaving their babies to be destroyed. What else could they do?

The sky to the east had turned from black to gray and the stars were fading. The moon was just a sliver of silver hanging low on the horizon. In minutes, the morning sunshine would burst forth through the trees.

In the valley just to the east of the explosion, five people were beginning to rub their eyes sleepily.

"Dad?"

"Yes, Kitten?"

"I smell turtle soup."

"Me, too," agreed Sally. "I'm hungry. Let's get up."

"Dad, can we build a fire and have biscuits?"

"Yeah, we want biscuits with the turtle soup."

Dad stretched and yawned. "I think not. We have things to do today and we need our time. Out of the bed, everyone. You can have crackers with your soup."

Later, the large helicopter followed the valley for a mile, then began to climb. The ridge of mountains was high above them and as the chopper reached the crest, a plume of smoke greeted them.

A little farther over the mountain, rolling clouds of black came into sight. Then the red tongues of flame cut through the dark smoke as the fire raged on.

"Look, Dad! Fire!"

"Yeah, Dad, the whole valley is on fire!"

"Did lightning cause it?"

"It couldn't have. There wasn't a storm."

"Was it careless campers?"

"How would Dad know? He was asleep with us."

"But he might know. Oh, look at our tent! The fire burned around it but didn't burn it up because it was on the rock. Look, Dad!"

The helicopter arose above the flames and smoke and settled down on the rock beside the tent. The hillside was blackened and smoky and dead fallen logs smoldered and blazed. Mr. Wentworth picked up his radio to call for help. The speaking range was certain to be too far for the radio, but he could try.

That instant a light plane came up the valley, circled and made another pass. Out of the plane dropped several small, dark dots that grew larger and suddenly blossomed into parachutes. They settled to the ground as the plane came around again, dropping more firefighting equipment.

The photographer put his radio away. The firefighters already knew about the fire.

Dennis ran to the tent. "The flashlight is still on, Dad. Those were really good batteries."

"Hey, Dad, the tent just about burned up. Look at all the holes in it."

"How come it to get all of the burn holes?"

By now everyone was inspecting the tent.

"The fire didn't do this," Mr. Wentworth decided.

"Then what?"

"It looks like bullet holes."

"Bullet holes!"

"How could that be?"

"Shall we take down the tent, Dad?" Dennis wondered.

"Not just yet. I think that tent just might be evidence. We'll see if we got a picture."

"Evidence?"

"Someone just tried to kill us, can't you see?"

"What did we do?"

"Dad, look at the camera."

The fire had burned close to the tripod and the camouflage cover has been scorched. The legs of the tripod were blackened, but the camera still stood firm.

"Do you think the film is all right?"

Many of the small trees were burned away now, giving a much better view of the pointed mountain which was no longer there. Darla stood staring at it for a few minutes before she nudged Sally.

"Look over there, Sally. Does that mountain look different or is it just my imagination."

Sally looked. "Hey, it looks like a giant took a bite out of the side of it. Did it burn up?"

Now the boys and their father were looking toward the mountain.

"Dirt doesn't burn," sneered Danny.

"Then tell me what happened?"

Danny had no answer.

Dad turned toward the helicopter. "Pile in, kids. We're going down there. Dennis, take the camera. First we make a pass around the mountain, and you be ready to get good shots. If there is no trouble down there, perhaps we'll put down."

Dennis, camera in hand, had stationed himself at the window. They lowered into the blackened valley, past the small lake and around the hill. The fire had burned itself out, but a gaping hole was left in the mountain. It looked as though a huge giant shovel had taken away a scoop of dirt from the side of a pile, causing the dirt at the top of the heap to slide down.

Shiny metal containers were lying around, just tossed here and there. Some had rolled down the hill, their shiny cylinders outlined plainly against the black ground.

Mr. Wentworth circled the area twice with Dennis shooting film, then he put down on the top of a ledge. Large rocks and sliding dirt had covered over the grassy meadow.

"Now, listen everyone. Go slow and don't touch any of those cans," Dad warned as his passengers disappeared out of the chopper.

"It was an earthquake."

"On just one mountain?"

"Then what?"

"Landslide?"

"But what caused it?"

"The fire?"

"I don't think so."

"I think the mountain exploded."

"Exploded?"

"That's it. It exploded."

"But how?"

"Dad...?"

"Yes, you could be right. There could have been an explosion, but we don't know why," Dad answered.

They walked over to one of the metal containers. Part of its label had been ripped away, but there was enough left to see the black design indicating that it contained harmful chemical waste. Among the words still readable were "CAUSTIC ACID."

"Bad, isn't it, Dad?"

"Someone was very careless."

"On purpose."

"They just threw these cans out on the side of the mountain!"

"And then blew them up?"

"No, look, Dad! It was a big cave and the explosion filled it in."

"Yeah, look, it was blown up."

"See, there's part of the cave wall."

"Look over here. A can broke and yellowish stuff is running out."

"Guess what I see," Sally announced.

"What?"

"Look down there. Isn't that the pointed stone? Isn't that the one we saw in the picture?"

"It sure looks like it."

"Way down there?"

"See that dirt way up there on the mountain? That's just about where it was."

"And look at the trees it knocked down."

"But why!"

"Someone wanted to get rid of something?"

"Or hide it?"

"Way out here? That shouldn't be very hard. How many people ever come out here?"

"There's five of us and we're here now."

"What are we going to do, Dad?"

They turned toward the photographer, who was kneeling beside one of the cans, camera running. Then he carefully removed the torn paper label.

"Let's go, kids."

"Where?"

"First to Granite, and then on to Denver."

"Are we leaving our tent here?"

"Yes, we'll be back. Hurry, now."

They stopped in Granite just long enough to make a phone call, and then they were off again.

The representative from the Environmental Protection Agency was waiting for them at the airport. The official behind the desk examined the label and put the picture on the screen. It showed the parallel marks of the sled runners going into the cave. And there was a picture of a small tent on a moonlit hillside. A bubble helicopter approached, turned broadside and fired blazing bullets toward the tiny target with the flashlight inside. The bubble turned to the opposite side and fired another round, then it flew off into the valley, silhouetted against the moon.

There was a long space on the film showing only the lonely tent with the flashlight still burning. Then a small flame showed in the distance. Closer it came and higher the flames arose until finally it surrounded the tent. The flames died away and the tent remained.

Several frames of the film showing the bubble were printed onto hard copy and enhanced, making the light parts lighter and the dark parts darker. Numbers and letters appeared. The complete set of markings was visible as the chopper turned to get a better shot at the tent. Within seconds the computer furnished information.

"It's registered to Arthur 'Lefty' Sharp," the police lab attendant told them.

The torn label was easily traced to a local manufacturing plant. The EPA representative dialed the number.

"Tri-Market Chemical. How may I help you?... Yes, a Mr. Arthur Sharp and two associates were hired by us to dispose of chemical waste into the protected chemical dump... Receipts from the approved dump area? Why, yes, we have a receipt for every load. They are numbered 173A921 to 173A969. That would be the 47 completed trips, plus the one that went out today. Another one is being loaded right now... Sure, we can hold him. Shall we lock him up for you? No?... Then we'll just detain him out in the loading yard... Oh, no trouble at all. We're just glad to help... Then we'll expect to hear from you... Sure thing."

The uniformed security person hurried to the rear of the chemical plant and ran to the loading yard. He called to the helicopter pilot who was waiting for his release. "Sorry to detain you, Mr. Sharp, but we are going to be a few minutes longer with the papers. Could we offer you a cup of coffee inside? No? Then we'll hurry. Please bear with us."

Lefty Sharp leaned back in the pilot's seat for a little nap.

Elmer complained, "I don't like it. I just don't like it at all."

"But there ain't nothin' that can be done about it, so jist settle your feathers and rest."

"But still," insisted Elmer, "things that start going bad just keep on that way."

"Aw, that's got nothin' to do with nothin'. They're just slow gettin' around in there. Don't you go to gettin' the heebie-jeebies agin."

"I ain't got the heebie-jeebies. Didn't you never hear about bad things comin' in threes? We had them flower sniffers come around, then we had to blow up that last place before we was ready. Now this."

Lefty sighed. "Well, if you was to put it that way, them two things you jist mentioned is the same bad thing and that'd mean we got two more bad things comin'. How do you like that?"

"Oh, hush up."

Lefty had just closed his eyes again when the uniformed attendant returned with the necessary clearance papers.

"Sorry to detain you so long, Mr. Sharp," he apologized.

"Thank nothin' of it," said Lefty cheerfully, and within minutes he was buzzing away with his cargo. Expecting three bad things in a row was stupid. How did it ever get started, anyway? Just another nonsense saying. That small plane overhead had nothing to do with him. They were always buzzing around doing their thing. He had to get on out to the new hiding place and get off-loaded so he could get another load today.

Elmer fidgeted and cleared his throat. Several times he started to say something but changed his mind. So what if there was an airplane overhead that seemed to do a lot of circling? There was always a lot of small aircraft around the Denver area looking at hills and valleys. Most of them were flower sniffers and mushroom chompers. But somehow that didn't make him feel a lot better right now.

Bart waited at the new cave. He had finished planning the best way to stash the largest number of cans in this new, smaller cave, and now he sat down to wait for the bubble aircraft.

In the airplane overhead, the uniformed officer lifted the microphone. "This is Skyhawk to Turtledove 1. Proceed below mountaintop level to valley 17. Copy?"

"This is Turtledove 1 to Skyhawk. We copy."

"Skyhawk to Turtledove 2, go north to valley 16 and cross over at Pica Point. Go slow and stay open. Copy?"

"Turtledove 2 to Skyhawk. Roger."

The aircraft droned on, circling lazily overhead. Elmer was getting even more nervous.

"I got me this bad feelin'...."

"Ain't no surprise to me you got a bad feelin'. I'd have me a bad feelin', too, if I ate three cans of sardines and drank a quart of buttermilk."

Elmer did not answer. He wanted to tell Lefty to do something, but what would it be? If they weren't being followed, there was no trouble to be worried about. If they were being followed, it was too late to do anything now, and there was no way the tiny helicopter could get away after it had been spotted. He just sighed, closed his eyes and leaned back in his seat.

The message crackled through the radio, "Skyhawk to Turtledove 2. Accelerate to valley 1 and proceed south. Target is visible on the east side of the mountain from Marco Point. Copy?"

"Turtledove 2 to Skyhawk. We copy and will comply."

"Skyhawk to Turtledoves 1 and 2, it's your party now. We're going home! Good luck." With that, the small plane circled once more and headed back toward Denver.

The Wentworth helicopter settled down on the large flat rock on the top of the ridge.

"Change of plans. Boys, take down the tent and bring it on up here. Girls, repack those suitcases so we'll have a little more room in the chopper. We're headed home."

"Aw, Dad, let's go watch the cops catch those criminals."

"No, Danny, they don't need us in the way. We've done our part."

"Dad, why did that chemical company let those fellows hide that stuff in the caves instead of the safe disposal area?"

"They didn't know what was happening. They were receiving receipts from the disposal area, not knowing a book of receipts had been stolen."

"Did those men get a lot of money for doing that? They got all of the money they should have paid to the disposal site and the money for hauling it, too. It must have been a lot."

"They're going to have trouble spending it if they are in jail, huh?"

"What will those cans do to the dirt when they get rust holes? They are going to ruin the mountain, aren't they?"

"Yeah, and that stuff will wash down into the valley and kill the fish."

"And the turtles."

"And then it will be in the river."

"And then the ocean."

"And then every sea shore around the world?"

"All from one little spot in the mountains."

"All right, kids, pile in. I've changed my mind, and we're going over there. This would make a very good story for the people who are interested in taking care of nature. They should get a chance to see what can happen if we're not careful."

"Oh, boy, we talked him into it!"

"Dad?"

"What, Kitten?"

"They would have gotten away with it, at least for a longer time, if we had not taken a picture of that pointed rock, huh? And then we would have been gone on home if we hadn't gotten curious about that rock. Then we wouldn't have been here when the forest fire came if we hadn't wondered why that mountain kept getting smaller."

"That's right. This time we were lucky that it happened the way it did.

By afternoon, the bubble helicopter and its crew were apprehended and were in custody, and Montgomery Wentworth had his film and was ready to head home.

On the way back to Missouri, they would be photographing the stream that flowed east of the hill. They flew slowly over the trickle of water until it reached the upper part of the Arkansas River. The river started small and thin, collecting in pools and then spilling over in waterfalls, each one bigger than the last.

The little stream flowed down into Kansas, and the chopper set down beside it for the night.

Sally ran to the river and dipped up a cup of water. "Hey, look! I got some of the water that flowed off the rock on the mountain."

"How do you know it's the same water?"

"How do you know it isn't? It looks like it."

"Aw, water all looks the same."

"So it might be the same water."

They set up the stove and heated their canned chili and wieners. They sipped chocolate and thought about their Bible verses.

"I got one. 'The wicked shall be cut off.' I don't remember how it was used in the Bible, but it describes what happened to those men."

"You're right," agreed Dad, "but wicked people do not always get 'paid' for their wickedness in this life. A lot of times they think they're getting by with something, but the punishment will always come."

"I'm next," Darla announced. "David said, 'The clouds are God's footstool'. They could have been our footstool while we were flying on the top of the mountain."

"Dennis?"

"I'm thinking."

"Danny?"

"'Follow me and I will make you fishers of men.' If we act like Christ, we make others want to follow Him."

"Now, Dennis?"

"I got it. I can't remember exactly how it goes, but it's about the wise man who built his house on the rock so it wouldn't fall down when the storm came. Well, we set up our tent on the rock and it didn't burn up when the fire came."

"Very good. Mine is, 'Lo, I am with you always, even unto the ends of the earth'. No matter where we are, Christ is there, and that's a good thought to remember. Goodnight, kids."

It was about three months later when Sally and Darla turned on the Public Television Station to watch a film.

First they saw a lizard eat a spider who had caught a bug for his lunch. Then the lizard ate the bug.

Next there was a baby bird being fed in his nest by the mama bird.

A turtle thumped by, fell over, got back up and shuffled on.

A tiny white cloud drifted overhead. Then the clouds became black and thick, and lightning flashed out of them. A small fire started where the lightning flashed, and it burned until the rain came and put it out.

Next the film showed large water drops that fell on the rock and divided themselves, some flowing east and others flowing to the west.

The little bush growing from a crack in the rock leaned to the west and shed water from its pointed leaves, and the water poured to the west. A gust of wind whipped against the bush, blowing it to the east, and the water ran off its leaves and flowed to the east. Neat!

The camera followed one stream down the mountain, past a cave and under the trees until it joined other streams of water to form a blue lake in the valley.

Then the other stream was followed by the camera as it raced down the mountain and became the crystal pool with tiny fish and large turtles.

"Oh, look, Sally. There's our turtles!"

The pool overflowed into a stream that became the headwater of the Arkansas River. It flowed lazily through Kansas and cut through the corner of Oklahoma. At this point, it had been teamed up with an earlier Wentworth film and was followed on through Arkansas, all the way to the Mississippi and on to the Gulf. Small boats were sailing in the Gulf of Mexico as the film ended. The girls sighed and turned off the television.

"I really like that one," pronounced Darla approvingly, "but next week they'll show the one I don't like very well."

"Yeah, with cans laying all over and the mountain caves all blown up."

"Probably some of those cans are already rusted open."

"I just thought of something."

"What?"

"You know, if that poison had gotten in the water in the cave where Dennis fell in...? And if it was poison... well, then...?"

"Hmmm, you're right. And it could happen, because they'll never find all of those cans no matter how hard they look."

"I wonder how those men could think money was worth that much."

"I wonder where they are now."

"Jail, I hope."

"But for how long?"

"Not long enough, that's for sure."

Danny and Dennis were stretched out on the floor on their stomachs with the World Atlas before them.

"See, there's Africa. Now look for that little twisty river. Oh, there it is," Danny pointed.

"No, it's over here. And see how it's marked? Dad circled it with a pencil, but I know it's the next place we go to."

"Boy, oh boy, I can't wait!"

"I'm afraid you'll have to..." His brother answered sarcastically.

THE CASE OF THE TUMBLING TRIPLET

Darla Wentworth was very lonely. She sat at the kitchen table in her mobile home in Branson, Missouri and thought about loneliness. It was such a funny thing. No matter how many people were around, it was still possible to be lonely.

"Daddy?" she said in the direction of the open newspaper across the table.

"What, Kitten?" came her father's voice from behind the paper.

"Does the trip to Peru absolutely have to be right now?"

Mr. Wentworth put the paper aside. "Now, Kitten, you've asked me that question twice already. I'm telling you the truth. The Peruvian government set the date when we could have access to the temple ruins to make the film, and we must go when we have permission. Some things cannot be changed."

"But, Daddy, it just isn't fair."

"That's right. Life is full of things that do not seem fair. We have no promise of fairness...."

"I know that, but it's so much more fun for me when Sally can go along."

"I can understand that, little Kitten. That's why I schedule so many of my filming assignments when you and the boys are out of school."

"Really?"

"Certainly. Did you think that being a grownup keeps a person from being lonely?"

"I don't think I ever thought of it."

"Perhaps it would help you if you think about how other people feel. Since your mother died, all I have is my triplets—you, Danny and Dennis—and during the school year, I can't even have you with me."

"Hmmmm. I see what you mean. It's just that sometimes it seems like the boys don't really want me around. All they want is each other."

"Possibly you're just being too sensitive. You're growing up, and boys and girls can be different in the things they like to do. It could be that it is not so much a matter of them not wanting you, but of you not wanting to be around them, and that is not their fault. I know you like having Sally along, but she has a family, too, and they have a right to keep her with them sometimes. We'll have lots of pictures to show her, and perhaps she'll get to go next time."

"All right, Dad. I'll get started packing."

As Darla went down the hall, she could hear her brothers talking excitedly.

"See here," Danny pointed out. "This book says you can be in the hot climate down on the coast and, on the same day, be in the windy, cold and freezing mountains."

"I know. It seems like it would be hotter on the mountains because they are so tall, and they would be a lot nearer to the sun," Dennis agreed.

"Yeah, but it doesn't work that way. It has something to do with the weight of the air. Up on the mountain, the air seems to be thinner, so it doesn't hold the sun's heat as well as when it's heavier, like down in the valley."

"That sounds funny. Heavy air! Like if I had a bucket of heavy air, that I couldn't lift because it was so heavy. I'd say, 'Here, Danny, help me lift this bucket full of air!'"

"I'd say, 'No, I'm too busy! Just pour out some of your heavy air if you have trouble lifting it.'"

They laughed together at their joke and Darla, in the next room, stretched out on her bed and stared at the ceiling. There would be plenty of time this evening to do the packing. Right now, she had to figure out a way to get out of her dreary mood. Dad was counting on her.

Let's see, now. Boots, thermal underwear, insulated coveralls for sleeping in. The snake bite kit, the bug cream, alcohol for cleansing wounds, and aspirin in case of aching teeth. What else? Cotton balls, iodine, adhesive tape and all the other things required for a safe camping trip. They would be living out of the helicopter for three days.

Danny tromped noisily down the hall with the tent. "Get the bedrolls, Dennis, will you?"

Darla turned her thoughts away. There was more to think about, like the food box. Somehow, it had seemed to become her job to pack the food. They would need to take extra hot chocolate because of the weather. Fig and date bars were good for snacking. Canned stew was easy, so they would need a lot of crackers.

She sighed as she remembered what her father had told her when she complained about always having to pack the food. "Sometimes we get stuck with duties just because we perform them well," he had told her. Oh, well... she wasn't sure she would trust the boys to remember everything, anyway.

So, on with the food. How about canned chicken noodle soup to eat with the canned ham sandwiches? Soup was very good for warming the tummy. Also, there were sloppy joes for the third day. Or maybe the sloppy joes should be for the first day, so the buns wouldn't get stale. They would stay fresh for only three days. That was what Dad had said, but what if something happened and they stayed four days? No, the schedule and the permission from the government was for three days.

Still... it wouldn't hurt to put in two extra cans of corned beef and some onion flakes. Heated together, they made good, hearty sandwiches. Or, if she also put in a package of dehydrated potatoes, they could have corned beef hash, if there was time to cook it.

Well, now that everything was figured out, she might just as well get up and get busy. Food doesn't pack itself.

Professor Andrew McConnell, teacher of history, specializing in South American civilizations, checked his packing list one more time before snapping the suitcase shut. Extra warm socks, heavy boots, insulated coveralls because of the cold... what else?

A shiver of excitement passed over him. Here he was, finally going to see the land and people he had spent so many years teaching about.

Finally, he would be able to put away the slightly guilty feeling he always had when he taught students about a place he had never been able to visit. Likely the textbooks were correct, but how could he know for sure? Now he would know, and his lessons would be so much better! Permission had been granted to spend time in the modern cities and to travel to the ancient ruins. Guides had been arranged for him, possibly because of his age and his inability to climb extensively. In addition, due to the artificial leg he must use, he was given extra attention. Finally, at last, he was going!

Dr. and Mrs. McConnell took a taxi to the airport, where the powerful silver wings of the airplane lifted him into the sky and circled, turning its nose to the south.

Finally, and certainly better late than never, Dr. McConnell was to meet the South American people, descendants of the temple builders. He would see for himself how the current civilizations existed on the high, cold and windswept mountains... how they grew their crops... how they lived and what they talked about. Finally, he was going!

Danny thumbed through the pages of the information brochure. "These Indians didn't use arrows like Native Americans."

"What did they hunt with?"

"Clubs and sometimes blow guns, it says here."

"I wish I had a blow gun."

"Maybe we can get one. Or maybe we can learn how to make them."

"What do they blow?"

"I don't know yet. Let's read."

After that, there was no sound except for the turning of pages.

Darla selected the packages and cans of food and packed them expertly in the food box. They must be placed just the right way, or they took up too much room. The square cans of corned beef took up such a little space that she put in a third one. Around and between everything, she wedged envelopes of hot chocolate mix and packets of ground coffee for her dad.

There was a little space left. What else? Ah, the crunchy, light, dried banana flakes would be perfect for snacks. There. All done. Someone would have to help her carry it to the van.

"Dad?"

"What, Kitten?"

"The food box is ready. Shall we take it out now?"

"I suspect so. Everything else is packed."

They lifted the box by its well-worn handles and carried it between them to the van. It was dark now, and they could barely see well enough to slide the box into its place among the piles of gear. They worked the bulky box into place and closed the door of the van just as a bright light illuminated the yard. The headlights of a car shone to the end of the driveway as the car turned toward them.

"Now who could that be, this time of the night?" Darla wondered.

"It seems we shall soon see," responded her father, as the car door burst open and a running figure appeared in the glare of the headlights.

"Wait for me! Wait for me!" yelled Sally, dragging her sleeping bag and other gear as she ran.

"Sally! What happened?" demanded Darla, running to help her.

"I'll tell you later," she puffed breathlessly. "Oh, I can tell you now. I was so afraid God wouldn't know how early Uncle Monty would be leaving for the airport."

"God?"

"Yeah. No one else listened when I explained how badly I wanted to go to Peru."

"But God did?"

"Sure. He's the one who let Uncle Bill win the tickets for two couples to go on a cruise that doesn't allow kids along. Mom and Dad are going with them and I can go with you. See?"

"Sure," Darla agreed. Anyone could see that.

"But, Darla?" came Sally's worried question.

"What?"

"Did you pack enough food for me? I told God I had to get over here before the food box was packed, but He didn't listen."

"Sure He did. He told me to pack for you. There's plenty."

The lights of the car had disappeared down the lane and out of the mobile home park.

"All right, girls," came the stern voice of Mr. Wentworth. "Time for talk tomorrow. Right now you have to get some sleep. We leave in six hours."

"Six hours! Just think of it!"

"Let's hurry and get to sleep so it will come quicker."

From the airport in Phoenix, Arizona, the huge airliner lifted off the runway with Dr. Andrew McConnell aboard. Mrs. McConnell waved until the airplane was a dark speck that disappeared into the blue sky. She hoped his trip was a success so he would come back soon. It was such a worry to see him go off this way.

Dr. McConnell looked out the window of the liner at the clouds and counted the hours until he would be exploring and photographing the lands he had been teaching about for so many years.

At Lima, Peru, he boarded the little train that took him up the precarious trail of railroad tracks, waving and wobbling along the edge of the mountains. He passed through the villages, taking pictures of the colorful market places and of the noisy groups of playing children.

At the peak of the mountain, he met with Thurpa and Manco, who would guide him among the ancient ruins. He had carefully learned the words necessary to communicate with the guides during the hike through the jungle and the overnight stay among the ancient idols and the crumbling temples.

The trek into the jungle was a difficult one, even with two good legs, but the old professor managed to keep up with the guides. The sun was low when they reached the first temple ruins of their destination. The guides made a brush shelter for him and prepared his insect net for the night. All around him were the stone walls and leaning pillars he had come so far to see... the wonderful architecture erected by the ancient Inca civilization, just waiting here for his visit.

He took a lot of pictures in the fading light and went to bed to wait, sleeplessly, for the morning light. There were carvings and pillars covered with designs, and he especially wanted pictures of the stone idol for whom the leaning temple had been built. The idol itself was ancient, weathered and crumbling but was still magnificently surrounded with history.

At the airport in Branson, Missouri, the little Beechking jet taxied to the runway and waited for the tower to give permission to take off.

"Tower to Beechking ICU2. Come in."

"Beechking ICU2 to Tower. Acknowledge."

"Tower to Beechking ICU2. You are clear for Runway one four. Have a good flight."

"Beechking ICU2 to Tower. Roger and thank you. Beechking out."

The pilot of the jet sped down the runway and nosed into the darkness of the morning sky. He turned up the volume of his speaker and music filled the cockpit. They were off. The pilot stared from the dark sky to the lighted instrument panel and back again, and behind him were his four passengers.

"It's too dark to play checkers," Dennis complained. "What'll we do?"

"We could eat."

"Good idea. Who has the granola bars?"

"You have."

"Oh, that's what was in the sack. Anyone want one?"

"Yeah, and I'll swap you an orange juice for a bar."

The wax box of orange drink sailed across the back of the seat, and a granola bar was tossed in the opposite direction.

"Me, too," called someone else, and more food flew overhead.

"I'll take a bar to Dad."

"Take him juice, too."

"No, he'll want coffee. He has his thermos up there with him."

Clusters of lights below them indicated small towns. Eureka Springs, Arkansas, then Rogers, Arkansas. Then came the city of Fayetteville.

By the time they passed over the tiny town of Mountainburg, with its twin mountain lakes, daylight had arrived and a checker game was in progress.

"It's my turn."

"You already played."

"No, I changed my mind."

"You can't do that."

"I did."

"Put that checker back."

"No."

"Then I will. Yuck! It's sticky. What's on this checker?"

"Orange juice."

"Dennis, did you spill orange juice?"

"Only a little."

"This checker is all sticky."

"Then leave it alone. The stickiness was not bothering me."

"Yeah, but you got the board messy."

"I know. But now the checkers won't slide off so bad when we bump the board."

"Hey, you're right."

"Let's pour some more juice on it."

"Dennis! Dad, make...."

"Aw, I was just joking."

"Who's turn was it?"

"I forgot."

"Then let's start over. Heads or tails?"

"Tails."

"Heads. I get to play first."

Sally and Darla had dozed off for a while, but now as the jet passed over the town of Alma, Arkansas, they aroused.

The pilot picked up his mike.

"Beechking ICU2 to Fort Smith Tower."

"Fort Smith Tower. Come in."

"Beechking ICU2 passing through on schedule to Dallas World Airport."

"Acknowledge, Beechking ICU2. Happy landing."

The Arkansas River threaded its way through the city of Fort Smith, its surface silver in the morning light. South of Fort Smith, they turned to the southwest, setting a course for Dallas, Texas. The jet carrying the pilot-photographer and his passengers threaded its way through the sky, checking in with towns, cities, and airports, finally reaching Lima, Peru.

It was dark when they put down at the airport in Peru. Their first night in Peru would be spent in the jet, bedrolls spread here and there. It was time for evening devotions.

"After all these hours in the plane, everyone should be able to remember a very good verse for devotions."

"We don't have any hot chocolate."

"We can't make it. We can't use the stove in an enclosed place. That's what the directions say. It could make dangerous fumes."

"I know that. I just said we didn't have any. Devotions are easier to think of if I have hot chocolate."

"Kids, get to thinking. Danny?"

"I'm ready. 'Where your treasure is, there will your heart be, also.' I don't know what it means, but I thought of it because the temples in Peru are considered treasures. What does it mean?"

"That verse means that the things of God should be our treasures, and if they are not, then we are putting other things before God. God wants to be first in our lives. Darla?"

"I'm ready. 'Be sure your sins will find you out.' I thought of that because of Danny's verse and about the man who stole treasures out of Jericho, and made Joshua lose a battle."

"Good. Sally?"

"I'm thinking of 'Pride goeth before destruction'. I'm proud of my family and my country, but I don't think that's what the verse means."

"You're right, Sally. Dennis?"

"How about, 'Thou shalt put no other Gods before me'. That fits with Danny's verse, doesn't it?"

"It sure does. God expects our whole life to be centered around Him, but He returns the favor when He says 'I will give my angels charge over you, to keep you in all your ways'. So, off to sleep with all of you. Tomorrow will be an early day."

So, in the early morning light, they moved their supplies and gear to the waiting rented helicopter. When packed, it would take them to the mountain peak where there was no airstrip. The jet would have to wait at the airport to take them home.

The rented chopper was a big one with two props, very much like one they had in Missouri. The gear was stowed away, and the maps of the Peruvian Andes Mountain Range was spread out before them.

The photographer explained, "First we go directly to Lake Titicaca. One of the islands in the lake has a temple we'll want to film."

"Can we land on the island, Dad?"

"I plan to, Danny. That's one of the advantages of a chopper. They require no special place to land. Then we'll go down to the valley to the cluster of temple ruins. There's so many of them down there, and they're spread out, so they'll take all the rest of our time."

"That Lake Titicaca is a really big one, isn't it, Uncle Monty? I read that it was the highest large lake in the world."

"Yes, Sally, it's a very big one. Lakes are usually in valleys, but this one is at the tip top of the mountain range."

"How did it get up there?"

"Someone moved it up, bucket by bucket," Dennis explained helpfully.

"Did not! How, Dad?"

"The best explanation seems to be that at one time it was at ocean level but was lifted as the mountain range arose from the pressure of the tectonic plates against the western shore of South America. Somehow, the mountain must have been lifted as a single, complete piece instead of crumbling and letting the water drain out, as would be expected. Anyway, the lake is up there, and we're going to take a look at it."

"It sure is hot here, Dad. Can we go swiming in the lake when we get up there?"

"I don't think so, son. It will be too cold on the mountain."

"I don't mind. Can we?"

"We'll see. Who cooks dinner tonight? Have you decided? No? Then we'll do it now. Boys, heads or tails?"

"Heads."

"Heads have it. You have the first day, and we'll be very hungry, so be prepared to fix plenty. Buckle your seat belts and here we go."

The helicopter lifted off the airport runway and climbed into the sky over the modern city of Lima, Peru. It followed the coast for a few miles, then turned and began to climb into the mountains. When possible, they flew between mountain peaks because of the strong, fierce wind that blew across the mountaintops.

The steep mountainsides were terraced with stone walls to make small, flat gardens for corn, squash and pumpkin patches. Tiny villages, actually just clusters of huts, nestled in the mountain valleys near the terraced gardens.

Brightly-dressed Peruvians cared for their gardens and their flocks of animals, now seen dotted among the hills. Strange animals they were, looking like a cross between a sheep and a camel, but the Peruvian llamas were very strong and could carry heavy loads up the steep hills. They had no shortness of breath as a donkey would have, and they climbed the hills and mountains that seemed tall enough to reach into the clouds.

The chopper circled a village and set down on a flat stretch of road. The llamas stopped nibbling the grass and turned to look at the noisy machine. The whir of the camera made movie stars of them while they twitched their ears and wiggled their noses. Then the noisy aircraft continued to climb up and over the trees toward the cluster of clouds at the top of the mountain.

"Look at the mountain," shouted Dennis, above the noise of the chopper. "It reaches all the way into the sky, just like the plant in the JACK AND THE BEANSTALK book."

"How are we going to find where we're going?"

"We have a map, Danny."

"But we can't see the ground to see where we are."

"Dad can find anything. He'll find the island."

"Yeah, but you forgot one thing."

"What?"

"Even if we find the island, how can we take pictures? All we would get is pictures of the inside of a cloud."

"Oh! That's right!"

"Dad?"

"What, Danny?"

"Do we get more time from the government if the weather messes us up?"

"We sure do, but, of course, we would have to go back to the valley and re-provision our food box. Chances are that the clouds will go away, or at least move over."

At that moment, the helicopter slipped inside the chilly whiteness of the cloud and everything below them disappeared. The green of the garden strips and the brown of the climbing trails were instantly gone. The blues of the sky and the distant mountain peaks were not visible... only the white of the cloud. The soft mist of the cloud enclosed them like a blanket, making the sound of the propeller blades seem even louder.

"Hey, Dad?" Darla called.

"Yes, Kitten?"

"It seems like we're flying through a marshmallow, doesn't it? But, Dad, I'm sort of worried."

"About what?"

"How do we keep from running into the side of a mountain?"

"Well, Kitten, that could be a problem, but it isn't as bad as it might seem. The wind is very strong as it blows up the mountain. I can tell from the force of the wind against the chopper when we're getting close to the mountain, and I can lift a little more. There's no reason for you to worry."

"Are you saying the wind is helping us?"

"Yes, this time it is. Also, it may help to clear away the clouds when we get there."

"Maybe the sun will come out."

"It can't."

"It might."

"No, it can't. The sun doesn't do anything. The earth goes around the sun. You mean maybe the clouds will get out of the way so we can see the sun," Danny explained.

"All right, smarty, then why do we say it's sunrise when we see the sun in the morning? Why don't we call it an 'earth-lower' instead of a 'sunrise'?"

"Because we're dumb, I guess."

"Then 'sunset' would be 'earth-rise', wouldn't it? We would say, 'My, what a beautiful earth-rise'."

"The clouds got thicker, didn't they, Dad? Now they're like whipped cream."

"No, they're like marshmallows."

"Whipped cream."

"Marshmallows."

"Whipped cream."

The chopper pilot called to his passengers, "That's enough, kids."

"Dad, how much farther is it to the top of the mountain?"

"Quite a way. Probably another half hour."

"Are the clouds getting thinner?"

"I don't think so."

The chopper continued to climb up into the whiteness.

"Brrrr," complained Dennis. "I sure wish it was warmer. I wanted to go swimming in that lake."

"I thought you might change your mind," Dad reminded him.

Down the mountainside near the temples, the old professor was awakened by the screaming of the colored birds in the trees and the raucous chattering of the monkeys. He rubbed his eyes at the strange sound, then realized where he was, and that he had been able to sleep in spite of his excitement.

Eager anticipation settled around him like a warm blanket, and the smell of the jungle flowers filled his lungs. Ah, the Andes! The beautiful mountains, the jungle, the temples! He wanted to see everything all at once.

He peered out of the shelter his guides had made for him, and all was quiet except for the snoring of his guides as they still slept nearby. Surely they should be getting up so the exploring could get started.

On second thought, why not let them sleep while he went for a first look at the temples alone? They were very close nearby, and there would be no chance of getting lost, so why would he need the guides? As he thought more about it, he realized he would prefer to be alone, just himself and the history he loved so well.

Quietly he dressed, strapping his prosthetic leg into place. Eager excitement made his heart pound like a drum, and his excited fingers could hardly work the buckles and buttons fast enough.

He stepped from the shelter and looked around him. Which way would he go first? He saw unbelievable wonders in every direction.

Hmmmm, how about that old temple that seemed to be leaning back toward the mountain? He would go and see why it was leaning. A rockslide? An earthquake? Tree roots in the foundation? He would go and see.

There were pieces of broken walls all around him, and some columns were cracked and broken and no longer supported a roof. There were fragments of idols and statues that had been broken (by what?), and they were weathered by many summers and winters. Such fascinating puzzles and wonders around him! There would be time for everything, but first, the leaning temple.

The lush vegetation was dripping wet from the moisture condensed through the night, and it swung wetly against him, drenching his clothing with dew. The grass was soaked, and the stones were moss-covered and slippery as the doctor picked his way through them toward the ancient, moss-covered stones of the temple.

Weathered stone idols stared with unseeing eyes as he walked past. If they knew the secrets of the leaning temple, they were telling no one. They held their cracked and broken arms against their sides and stood solidly, their feet buried in decades of mud and jungle plants. Vines circled the idols and clung with their green tendrils as they climbed up to the head and neck of some of the taller stone carvings. Slippery moss grew in the shade of the vines.

Dr. McConnell held his notebook high so the wet leaves would not spoil the paper and smear his ink. He would want to make sketches and notes to match the photographs he would make later. The guides were still asleep, and there was no need to wake them yet. Just now, he preferred to be alone with his thoughts.

At the base of the leaning temple, he could see where the heavy stone wall had sunk into the earth, causing cracks to form in the crumbling masonry. Some of the rocks had pulled away from the foundation, leaving gaping fissures and holes. Brilliant jungle birds screamed and fluttered overhead, and a red and yellow snake looped from a vine over his head.

The doctor touched the stones of the temple lovingly... almost reverently. What hands had placed this stone? With his finger, he traced the mortar holding the rocks together, wondering what kind of people had created the mixture of this mortar. And where had the ingredients for the mixture come from? It was crumbling now, but it had held these stones together for centuries!

He took a step closer. Stooping low, he stepped between the broken sides of the arched door. When his eyes became accustomed to the dimness, he saw the large carved idol, about which he had only read. Its arms were outstretched as though to welcome Dr. McConnell to the temple.

The smile of the stone god had been frozen into the stone by the carver. Short, stubby legs were planted firmly on a tilting stone platform, broken and crumbling with age. Beyond the idol was a hole in the ground. It was odd, of course, because why would anyone dig into the hard dirt floor of the temple? Why would they dig? What were they looking for?

He took a step closer to the stone figure. Ah, there at the feet of the idol was a different kind of stone! It was flat like a doormat, and it was set unevenly. The doctor took another step and touched the flat rock with his shoe. It did not move. He leaned over and pushed with both hands.

Suddenly, the slippery stone began to slide across the moss-covered platform, revealing a dark hole beneath it. Sacrifices to the idol! That's what the hole was for! Sacrifices of gold and silver, perhaps food or small animals would be laid at the feet of the idol to be swallowed up by the black hole. Strange! Very strange! Why would people offer things of value to a stone figure that had been carved by themselves? What could make them feel that it had power?

He took another careful step toward the black hole. There was no way to know how deep it was, but this was certainly the reason for the other hole. Treasure hunters hoped to intercept the first pit and reach in to get the treasures that had been offered to the idol. How wonderfully interesting! It was fascinating to think what wondrous things would have been offered to such an important idol as this one seemed to be.

Then the treasure hunters came to steal the treasures away. What would they have been? He would never know.

Above him, through the window of the crumbling temple, swung a chattering monkey. The sudden sound startled the professor, and he turned to look. Momentarily off balance, he took a small sliding step onto the mossy platform.

In a flash, his foot slipped, and he skidded down the sloping rock toward the idol. He reached for the outstretched stone hands of the idol, but he was sliding too fast. Head first, he fell into the dark blackness of the sacrifice hole, catching his foot on the cover stone, which held it firmly.

There, head down, he hung in the hole with the smooth, slippery sides. He felt along the sides of the hole for a stone or root to grasp and draw himself back up, but there were none.

The foot held him firmly and without pain, because it was his prosthetic leg, held by a strap around his waist. At first he was careful to move slowly so the foot would not be jiggled loose, knowing that if his foot slipped he would fall head-first into the depth of the hole.

That is what he did at first, but very soon, his blood began to run to his head, making him dizzy. He would soon be unconscious if he hung there upside down. What now? Die of hanging upside down, or drop into the unknown blackness below him? What a choice!

What was down there? Likely there was water! Surely snakes? What else? Then he began to wonder how far it was to the bottom, because certainly he would be forced to let himself down.

It was hard to think. He could not crawl out, so there was nothing else to do. He reached upward to the belt around his waist that held his leg in place. Carefully, he unbuckled the belt. He knew he was much too far from his guides to be heard, but he yelled anyway.

"Thurpa! Manco!" He waited, knowing they could not have heard him even if they were awake, which they probably were not.

Finally, he forced himself to pull the leather strap from the buckle and he fell, head first, down the hole, leaving his leg caught and still hanging above him. Into the soft mud at the bottom of the hole he fell, and an instant later, the leg came tumbling down into the hole after him, hitting him on the head.

For a while he lay, unable to think clearly, but then the coolness of the mud in the hole brought him back to consciousness. Somewhat revived, he looked up into the blackness and began to call loudly.

"HELP! COME HELP ME!" he called until he was too hoarse to yell any louder than a whisper. He felt the sides of the chute, but they were coated with slippery moss and mud, and he could not even see the top of the hole.

"HELP!" he called hoarsely.

Outside the temple, the sun was shining warmly through the leaves of the trees. Thurpa, warm and rested, stretched and yawned and nudged Manco with his foot.

"Wake up," he commanded and watched while his friend rubbed the sleep sand from his eyes.

"American?" he asked.

"Gone," was the reply. "Empty hut."

"We will find him so he can see what he wants to see, and we can get the money and go home."

"Yes. AMERICAN! SENOR!"

"SENOR AMERICAN!" Manco joined in. Still no response.

"Gone. We find him. With one leg, he will be near."

"With one leg he can walk fast, remember?"

"But why would he go fast? Here is what he came to see."

"Then we go look around. First the temple."

The guides paused at the doorway and stared into the dim light of the temple. The stone idol smiled at them over his extended hands.

"No American," decided Thurpa.

"Then where?"

"Ask the idol. Could be he knows."

"Dumb idol has no words," chuckled Manco. "Where is the American, old idol?"

At that moment, the hoarse voice of Dr. McConnell came from the hole.

"Please," the cracked voice whispered. "Please hear me."

Thurpa and Manco looked at each other and then back to the idol, their eyes wide and frightened. The voice came again. The words meant nothing to them, and the sound was eerie and evil-sounding.

"I'm in here. Please listen."

The guides edged backward out of the door.

"Please hear me," came the strange voice of the 'idol'.

The two guides turned and ran into the jungle, not stopping until several miles were between them and the temple, and the frightening talking idol.

At what they thought to be a safe distance, they sat down to rest in the shade. Thurpa scratched his head thoughtfully. "I know they say, in the stories the old ones tell, that stone idols speak, but I would never believe."

"But now you hear with your ears. What would he say if we would stay to listen?"

"I don't know what he would say," admitted Thurpa, "and I don't want to know."

"But I know," Manco insisted.

"What would the idol say?"

"He would say, 'I swallowed the American and I wait to swallow you now'. That's what he would say."

"But we ran away."

"No good. He knows our names."

"Then we change our names."

"More than that, we change our looks."

"Our looks?"

"Like this," demonstrated Manco as he rubbed his face with red clay.

Thurpa took a handful of the clay and smeared it on his cheeks. "Then we run away. The idol would know our village, so we run away."

Manco nodded agreement, and they both ran, disappearing into the jungle. They left the voice of the 'idol' far behind them, still pleading, "Please listen to me," but there was no one to hear. The stone idol smiled, but his stone ears heard nothing.

Finally, the voice was silent.

The helicopter, with two noisy propellers on the outside and four noisy passengers inside, climbed to the peak of the cloud-topped mountain.

"I'm hungry," announced Sally. "Who has the granola bars?"

"They're right behind you."

"Where?"

"In that sack."

"But I've been sitting on that sack," insisted Sally.

"Maybe so, but that's where the bars are."

Sally reached into the sack and took out a package. Instead of a hard, crunchy, square bar of nuts and grain, she held a sack of crumbles.

"Oh, look," she wailed. "They're just cumbs!"

"All of them?" Dennis asked, concerned.

"Yes, all of them," assured Darla.

"I guess we're lucky to have crumbs left, with Sally sitting on them for hours."

"They'll taste the same. Everything's still in the wrapper."

"Hand me one, and I'll be the judge of that."

"Watch out! You're pouring them down my neck!"

"Dad?"

"Yes, Danny?"

"The clouds aren't going away, are they?"

"Possibly not, but we still have several miles to go. We'll fly on out over the island."

The chilling moisture of the clouds was all around them, enclosing the helicopter inside its whiteness. Below them, the blue of Lake Titicaca could not be seen, and certainly the island in the lake was not visible, either.

"So much for filming the temple," announced Dennis.

"We could wait a while. Remember, you wanted to go swimming?"

"I changed my mind."

"What can we do, Uncle Monty?" Sally wondered.

"Well, Sally, we could wait a while and hope the clouds will lift off the lake, or we can go back down the mountain to the temples."

"Let's wait," suggested Darla. "I'm tired of flying."

"Me, too," agreed Sally.

"How long would we wait, Dad?"

"Dad doesn't know. You heard him."

"I mean how long would we wait to see if it was going to get better?"

"I'm cold."

"Is it warm down at the other temple?"

"I think so."

"Then let's go." suggested Darla. "This chopper is too little for all of us to wait in, and there is no other place that's warm."

"Yeah, let's go."

"I'm hungry."

"Have another sack of granola."

"What are we going to do, Dad?"

"He's turning around. See?"

"All I see is a cloud, and we're right in the middle of it."

"Hand me a sack of granola crumbs, please."

"We're going back down the hill. I hope we get there by dinnertime."

"How long will it take, Dad?"

"Dad's busy. I have the map, and we can figure it out."

"I'm thirsty."

"You can't have a drink of water."

"Yes, I can."

"No, you'll spill it. Dad...?"

"That's enough, kids. We'll set down for a minute so everyone can get a drink."

The chopper put down on the rocky shoreline of the lake, but the wide propellers continued to rotate with their loud "thwack, thwack, thwack" as the pilot and passengers jumped out of it to the ground.

"Brrrr," complained Darla as the lake breeze tore at her sweater.

"I'll race you to the lake and back," challenged Sally, and they were off.

While the boys took their turn at the water jug, the pilot looked at the land, sky and water, but mostly he looked at the cloud. The strong breeze blew ragged sheets of mist over the lake. No, there would be no pictures of the temple today. He did, however, take a number of shots of the fog as it was rolled about by the wind.

Within minutes, everyone was back inside the aircraft, and the propellers lifted them off the mountaintop into the sky.

"That hateful old cloud. It could have gone away for a day, and then we would be through up here."

"Yeah," agreed Darla. "What good are clouds, anyway?"

No one answered her question as the chopper began to work its way toward the edge of the mountain range, leaving the lake and the clouds far behind them on the mountain peak.

An hour later, Thurpa and Manco heard the "thwack, thwack thwack" of the chopper blades and stopped to stare at each other with frightened eyes. They crouched beneath a low rock ledge and hid from the strange flying creature that had been sent, no doubt, by the idol to search them out. They waited breathlessly as the chopper passed overhead, then they crept from their hiding place and continued to run. Any idol who could speak with a strange voice and words they could not understand could no doubt arrange for some frightful bird to search for them. Anyway, one could not be too careful.

Beneath the helicopter stretched miles of barren, rocky peaks and tiny trails. There were strips of trees and vines. The sun had broken through the clouds, bathing the earth in bright light, and the chopper instantly felt warmer. Sweaters were removed.

"Dad, may I take some of the pictures?" Danny asked.

"We'll see," answered the photographer.

"I'll take the little camera," he decided.

"I wanted that one," argued Dennis.

"Didn't we bring two?"

"I don't think so."

"Then we'll take turns. I'm first."

Surprisingly, Dennis agreed without complaint, mostly because he located the other smaller camera.

"We should be able to take some good pictures of birds," commented Darla.

"I want to take a bird home with me," Sally decided.

"I do, too, but you know what the permit said. All we can take away from Peru is pictures."

"Yeah. Mother wouldn't let me have a bird, anyway. She says they're too noisy in the morning when she wants to sleep."

The small aircraft had followed the mountain valleys and had swung around the rocky bluffs. Now, directly below them, were the ancient ruins. From the air, they could see the stone walls covered with vines. They saw steps and paths paved with stone in which trees had grown, pushing the stones aside.

As they drew closer, they saw more ruined buildings, many of them now just piles of stone. Centuries-old buildings had slid and leaned and finally fallen into heaps of carved stone, tied together in a web of vines.

"It's a good thing we came now. Look how that building is leaning. By next summer, it might fall over."

"Aw, they've been leaning that way for a hundred years. Didn't you know that?"

"Of course I did."

"Dad, where are you going to put down? I don't see a place big enough."

"I know where he's going. See that flat rock?"

"But that's so far away," observed Dennis.

"I'll race you back to the temple."

"All right," agreed Danny.

As the runners of the helicopter touched the solid firmness of the rock, the "thwack, thwack" of the whirring blades became silent.

The door burst open, and the passengers leaped down to the rock.

"I'll beat you!" threatened Dennis.

"Wait, boys," their father instructed. "Don't forget to watch for snakes and be careful."

Then they were off and running, and immediately the jungle foliage closed behind them.

"Oh, look at that vine! It's just covered with those gorgeous flowers. Let's go see if they smell good. You know how some jungle flowers look beautiful but stink like rotten eggs." Sally remembered.

"Yeah, I know, but that flower had to smell that way to attract the certain kind of insects that pollinated it. They were flies! Yuck! But if it smelled good, the flies wouldn't like it."

"Strange, isn't it?"

They hurried ahead in the direction the boys had disappeared. From behind them came the warning, "Girls, watch out for snakes."

Of course they would. They carefully pushed the plants aside so they could see where they stepped. There were other things to be avoided besides snakes. For instance, spiders, scorpions and centipedes.

The photographer brought up the rear, taking shots of this and that along the way. Even though the main purpose of the trip was for filming ancient Inca Indian temples, the other scenes could be used in the series, or even in other series. The flowers and insects would be parts of other documentaries. The rolling clouds over the windy lake would have a place in a documentary film on weather.

Danny and Dennis ran ahead, pushing aside the tall grass, ducking under low limbs and climbing over vines. The leaning temple was not far away, but it took a while to get there with the way the tendrils of the vines grabbed anything that went near them.

Fallen stones from old walls littered the ground, almost hidden in the grass, just waiting to trip the careless passerby.

Then the crumbling building was just ahead. Dense tree limbs had replaced the sunken roof, and the foundation was cracked and twisted by massive tree roots.

Vines covered parts of the structure, seeming to be trying to hold it together. The arched doorway was cracked and leaning, and the inside of the temple looked dim and inviting. Hesitantly, the boys took a few steps inside, seeming to forget they had been in a race.

"It's spooky," decided Danny.

"Worse than that. It's scary, but I got here first, so give me the camera."

"No, you'll have to catch me and take it away from me."

"Forget it. I'd rather explore the temple."

"Dennis, we really should wait for Dad...."

"No, he'll take forever to get here. You know how he films everything that creeps, walks or flies."

"But, Dennis...."

"Aw, I'm just going to look inside. No harm in that, is there?"

"Well, I...."

"Look, Dan, there's someone in there."

"What?"

"Come look for yourself. Oh, I see now. It's just a statue."

"Yeah, it's funny-looking. Look at the fat, stubby legs, and he looks like he's smiling."

"Maybe he's glad to see us."

"We're probably the first company he's had in years."

The boys leaned into the doorway, their eyes becoming accustomed to the dimness.

"Boy, its a mess in there! The jungle trees are pushing it in," Danny commented.

"Dan?"

"What?"

"Look at the statue's hands."

"Yeah, it looks like he's holding them out to welcome us, doesn't it?"

"More than that. Look what he's holding."

"Where?"

"Looped over his hand. It looks like something is hanging down."

"It sure does. What is it? Can you see?"

"Not very good," Dennis took another step and leaned into the temple.

"Dan, do you have our camera?"

"Sure, right here."

"Well, it looks like the statue has one just like it."

"It couldn't. It must be something else."

"No, Dan. It's a camera exactly like ours. Come over here and look."

Danny stepped closer to Dennis and leaned in as far as he could without entering the temple.

"Dennis, it can't be what it looks like. It looks shiny and new. I think we're seeing things."

"Yep, and I know what we're seeing. It's a camera, and I'm going to get it."

"No, Dennis, wait! You know what Dad said."

"But it's just a little way, and I'll come right back. You can see me all the way."

"No, Dennis...."

"I'll hurry." Then Dennis stepped through the door, scampering across the stone-littered floor of the temple.

The cool shade and the moisture had combined to create a strong, moldy smell, and the stones were slippery with moss. The surefooted Dennis picked his way skillfully over the fallen stones, hurrying toward the smiling idol.

"What is it, Dennis?" called Danny.

"A camera," answered Dennis. "Just like I thought it was. The carrying strap is hooked over the idol's thumb. I'm going to get it."

"But, Dennis...."

"Boy, it's spooky in here. I wish I had a flashlight."

"Dad has the light. Come back here, will you?"

"Sure. I just want to get the camera."

Danny looked behind him toward the helicopter. His father should be appearing any minute with the spotlight. Just then the fluttering wings of a bird overhead attracted his attention, and he looked up. He was watching the colorful bird, thinking how to aim the camera when he heard Dennis scream.

"DAANNNNYYYYY!"

"Dennis! What's wrong?" he yelled as he turned back to the temple. The temple was empty. Danny rubbed his eyes and looked again, but it was still empty.

"Help, Danny," came a voice echoing out of... nowhere? Actually, it seemed to be coming from the smiling stone statue.

"Dennis! Where are you?"

"In a hole," came Dennis' frightened voice.

"Are you all right?"

"I guess so. EEKKKK!"

"What's wrong, Dennis?"

"There's a foot down here!"

"Sure. You have two of them."

"But there's another one, and it has a leg hooked onto it."

"Just a foot and a leg? Are you sure?"

"Positive. Go get Dad. Hurry. I can't even see the top of the hole I fell into."

"All right, Dennis. Stay there and I'll hurry."

"I HAVE to stay here! I can't go anywhere."

Danny ran back toward the helicopter.

"DAD! DAD! HURRY!"

No answer.

Louder he called, "DAD! HURRY! DENNIS FELL IN A HOLE!"

"A what?" came the answer.

"A hole, Dad. Hurry."

"Was it a rock crevasse?" came the voice. "Can you see him?"

"No, Dad. It's a hole in the ground, but he's all right. Please hurry."

Of course, the photographer was hurrying! He ran through the vines, unbuckling the spotlight from his belt. The girls came stumbling through the vines, right behind him.

"Where is the hole, Danny?"

"In the old temple."

"Inside? Oh, Danny, you shouldn't go inside a building without a light."

"I didn't, Dad. It was Dennis. He wanted the camera."

"But...."

"The statue is holding a camera like ours. Dennis went after it."

"The statue? Oh, never mind. Let's hurry."

Danny paused at the broken archway door. "In there, Dad. DENNIS! DAD'S HERE!"

"Here, Dad," came a voice from the stone statue.

"Dennis?" called Dad. "I'm coming."

"Hurry, Dad. There's a foot down here, and I'm scared."

"A foot? There couldn't be a foot down there. Look, Danny, that statue is holding our camera. You said you didn't go inside."

"I didn't, Dad. I have our camera in my hand right now. That camera belongs to the statue. I tried to tell you it had a camera, and you told me 'never mind'."

"Hmmm."

The voice came from the ground. "Hurry, Dad. There's a foot down here, and I'm afraid to move because there might be something else. Besides, I think I sprained my wrist."

"Did you break it?" The photographer had reached the statue and was standing on the slippery stone, holding to the strong arm of the statue. From its stone thumb swung a camera exactly like the one Danny held.

"Danny," warned Dad, "be careful when you step on that platform, or you will be down there with Dennis. Those mossy rocks are as slick as greased glass."

"Hurry, Dad" came the voice from the blackness. "Help me out of here. This foot is scaring me."

"Now, Dennis," advised his father. "We're going to get you out. Don't be imagining there's a foot down there."

"But, Dad...."

His father interrupted him. "Now, son, how bad is your arm? Can you hold the rope?"

"I don't know, Dad. Maybe I can hold with my left hand."

"Now, Dennis, grab the rope and fasten it around your waist. No, put it under your arms. Can you do that?"

"I can't see the rope, Dad."

"Well, son, I'm shining the light for you, but there must be a sharp bend in the shaft if you can't see the light."

"I can't find the rope. I think it's too short."

"It's probably caught on the wall of the hole. Or a root or something. We'll pull it up and tie a rock to it so it will go down better. Are you still all right?"

"Yes, Dad, but hurry. There's...."

"I know, son. There's an extra foot down there with you."

Danny whispered, "Dad, what do you think the foot is?"

"Probably a strange-shaped rock," came the answer.

"Hurry, Dad," came the voice from below.

"All right, son. The rope is coming back down. I put a rock on the end. Start feeling for the rock."

"All right, Dad. I hear the rock on the sides of the hole."

"Can you reach it?"

"Almost."

"Do you have it now?"

There was silence.

"Dennis?"

"Let it down a little more, Dad. The wall is so slick I can't climb, and I can't quite reach it."

"That's all the rope we have, son. How much do you lack in being able to reach it?"

"I don't know. I can't see."

Danny whispered, "What can we do, Dad?"

His father answered sadly. "I don't know. Yet. My belt would add a little length but not much. There are a lot of vines, but I don't trust them. We may have to try them, though."

"I have a belt," offered Danny as he began to unbuckle it.

"Wait," said his dad. "Leave yours on. I have an idea I want to try first."

"What?"

"Wait right here. I want to find a strong pole."

In a minute he was back. He tied his belt to the end of the rope and attached the end of the Danny's foot.

"Now, son, I want you to lay down on your stomach and ease over to the hole. We'll thread this stick under your belt to keep you from falling in. See, now, the stick catches on the edge of the hole and will help me hold onto you. Now you are part of the rope. Let's see if it's long enough."

Danny eased over the hole and let his leg down. The ends of the stick caught on the sides of the mouth of the hole, holding him securely. His father stood back, holding to the belt.

"Dad?" came the voice from below. "Danny? Are you still there?"

"We're here, son. Watch for the rope. Tell me when you can feel it."

"All right, Dad. Hurry!" Then the voice came again. "I can touch it, Dad. Can you bring it down another few inches?"

"We'll try," came the answer.

Danny looked up. "Dad, we better look for a vine."

"No, I have one more idea. Danny, loosen your belt and bring it up under your arms. That will give him a few more inches."

"Yeah, and I'll be all the way in the hole."

"Are you afraid?"

"Yes, but I'll do it. Pull me up so I can."

"We'll find more sticks to put across the hole to be sure it's safe. Here, put your arms down to your side. I would do it, but I weigh too much more than you. As soon as we get him up high enough, I'll pull him up with the rope. Ready?"

"Yeah, Dad."

As Darla and Sally watched breathlessly from the archway door, Danny lowered himself into the black hole. Only his head and shoulders were in sight.

"I can reach it!" came the joyful announcement from below. "You can start pulling."

Danny reached for his father's hand. His father braced his feet firmly against the short strong legs of the stone statue, and he drew Danny toward him.

Slowly. Slowly. Now, Danny was up out of the hole to his waist. He turned and sat on the edge of the hole, braced against the short pole.

"Wait, Danny. Let me help you pull… now."

Slowly, Danny drew up his leg. "Boy, Dennis is heavy," he complained.

Dad reached down in the darkness and grasp the rope. "Dennis?"

"Yeah, Dad?" came from below.

"We're coming up fast now. Do you have a good hold?"

"Yeah, Dad."

Hand over hand, his dad pulled the rope, pausing for Dennis to secure his footing against the sides of the narrow hole. Danny stretched out on his stomach and watched. Then, in the light of the spotlight, the sole of a shoe appeared.

"Look, Dad! He's upside down!"

The foot came near the top of the hole. "Hurry, Dad!" Danny encouraged.

When Dennis was close enough to the top, he pushed the leg up and out of the hole, and it clattered noisily onto the stone platform.

The girls gasped, and Danny and his dad turned to stare at the leg lying beside them.

Next came the mud-smeared grin of Dennis. "I told you there was a foot down there with me."

His dad did not answer. He reached into the hole and grasped the belt Dennis had fastened just under his armpits and pulled him up to the stone platform. From the doorway, the girls sighed with relief; surely the frightening creature covered with black mud was Dennis.

Dennis crawled back from the hole.

"Dad, do you know what?"

"Probably not. What?"

"Dad, you're not going to believe me, but there's the body of a person down there."

"WHAT!"

"A body, Dad, and he's still warm. I think he's alive."

"Why didn't you tell me sooner?"

"I thought you wouldn't believe me. You didn't believe there was a foot down there when I told you."

"I'm sorry I didn't believe you, son. I thought perhaps you were so afraid that you were seeing things that weren't there."

"What are we going to do, Dad?"

"I'll have to go down there and get him out."

"I don't think so, Dad. There are places where the hole is very skinny. It could be hard for you to get through, and we couldn't get you out."

"You may be right, but we must do something."

Danny stood staring at the black hole. He didn't want to say what he was about to say.

"Dad?"

"Yes, Danny?"

At that moment, a loud, breathless shout came from outside the temple.

"Hey, Dad. We found a campsite. It has a brush shelter and a sleeping bag. Someone just left it here. And it's almost new!"

"Dad?" Danny began again. Shivers passed from his shoulders all the way down to his feet.

"Yes, Danny?"

"I'll go down to get him."

"But, son...."

"I'm all you've got, Dad. Dennis is tired and maybe has a broke arm, and Darla might not be able to lift him. Sally's too little. And Dennis says the hole is too small for you. It has to be me."

"But, Danny...."

"I'm going down, Dad."

"Wait, son. Let's decide how you'll get him up. How big is he, Dennis?"

"I don't know, Dad, but he isn't as big as you."

From the arched door, Darla called, "See the sleeping bag, Dad?"

"That's it!" shouted Dennis.

"That's what?" Darla demanded.

"That's how you can get him up! Tie him in the bag and pull the bag up. Good idea?"

"Very good idea. Toss it here, Darla. Get in here, Danny."

"Me?"

"Yes. I don't want you injured on the way down. Then we'd have two to bring up."

Danny was strapped securely into the heavy sleeping bag, and the rope was tied to the pillow portion. "I hope it doesn't tear."

"It shouldn't. It's made of heavy canvas, and it's new."

Feet first, Danny was lowered into the hole. The smell of damp, moldy earth was against his face. He sneezed and closed his eyes and mouth.

"Are you all right, Danny?"

"Yeah, Dad...."

Then his feet touched the bottom of the hole. The slippery mud slithered beneath his feet, making it hard to stand up. He unzipped the bag, being careful not to step on the body beside him. Was he dead or alive? Danny tried not to think about it. He felt around in the darkness.

"I have to have a light, Dad."

"Here it comes. Don't let it hit you."

Danny caught the spotlight as it came hurtling down the shaft, and he shone the light on the body. It was covered with the slippery, stinking mud. He sighed, wearily. How was he going to get this person into the bag?

Carefully, he touched the mud-smeared face. Still warm, so he was alive. That was good and not nearly so scary.

"Are you all right, Danny?"

"Yeah, Dad...."

Danny zipped the bag all the way open and flattened it the best he could. He lifted the man's foot into the bag. There was almost no room to work, because the bottom of the hole was about as big as a bathtub. He lifted the man's shoulders and trunk to put him in the bag. The man groaned but did not move.

"He's alive, Dad," Danny called. He heard his dad send Darla to the chopper for the first aid kit.

Danny sighed and scooted the man's shoulders a little farther. He was not a very big man, but the space was so cramped, Danny could hardly get a hold onto the slippery body. When he finally got the zipper edges together, they were too muddy to zip.

Now what? Sighing, he pulled off his tee shirt and turned it inside out, using the clean side to wipe the zipper. After a bit of scrubbing, he finally got it clean enough to zip up.

He was now sweating from the exertion. The man could not keep his one leg stiff, and he kept sliding to the foot of the bag. Dennis removed the man's belt and fastened it tightly to his waist around the outside of the bag, to hold him upright.

"Ready, Dad?"

"Ready, son. Here we go."

Danny crouched against the muddy wall to let the bag slide past him. Up it went, and small pebbles of rock and little chunks of mud came crumbling down on his head. He sat down tiredly, and felt the muddy water seep through his jeans. It suddenly felt freezing cold, but he was so tired he didn't care. Imagine! How would it be to be down here alone? Being down in this hole all alone with no one to get you out? And Dennis! He was down here, and he knew something was down here with him, but he didn't know what it was. No wonder he kept begging them to hurry.

Fright bumps began to rise on his arms and neck. What if Dad couldn't get him out? What would it be like to die down here? Was hell like this, only with fire instead of water?

"Dad!"

"What, Danny? Are you all right?"

"Yeah, Dad, but please hurry."

"Just a minute, son. We're taking him out of the bag."

Danny could hear the voices above him... near, but so very, very far. If someone didn't help him, he could never get out. He was totally dependent of the strength of someone else.

"Dad?"

"Ready, son. Here comes the bag back down to you."

"I'll just hold to it, and you can pull me up."

"No, Danny. Get in it. You're tired, and the bag is very slippery with mud. I want you to get inside it and zip it up. It will take a minute longer, but that way, I'll know you'll be safe."

"Sure, Dad." With an unbelievable relief, he felt the tension of the bag, and then he felt himself being lifted. Up and up. Relief made him shiver.

The muddy canvas of the bag plastered itself wetly against the bare skin of his back. He had forgotten to bring up the muddy tee shirt, but he wouldn't go back for it now. All he wanted was to get out of the hole. In his haste, he had pinched his finger in the zipper, but it only made him want to hurry faster.

The rope tightened around him as he felt himself being drawn upward. *Hold tight, Dad,* his mind kept saying. *Don't let me fall.* The short trip seemed to last forever.

Finally, up and out he came, and the dim light of the temple looked bright after the blackness from inside the hole. He blinked his eyes and looked around. His dad stood beside him to help with the zipper, as his slick, injured fingers did not want to work.

Danny crawled out of the dirty bag, wanting only to get out of the temple. One of the blankets from their camping gear was spread on the grass in the warm sunshine. The man with one leg lay on the blanket, looking at the girls and Dennis as though they were angels or at least some kind of beings from heaven who had appeared to help him.

The chopper lifted off the mountain, turned and headed toward the modern city of Lima, Peru. The floor space in the aircraft had been made into a bed, and the history teacher, somewhat cleaned from the mud, lay, still exhausted. It was time to turn him over to a hospital for rest and some nutritious food.

"I'm starving," Danny complained. "I was hungry when we left the lake, and it's worse now."

"Dad, can we eat in Lima? At a real cafe or something?"

"I can't wait that long. What do we have here?"

"No granola. There's crackers. Oh, I know! We have dried banana chips."

A voice came from the front of the chopper. "No crackers or dried chips, because there will be no water stops. We can't afford the time."

"Peanut butter?"

"Without crackers?"

"Is there a law that says peanut butter has to be eaten with crackers?"

"Hand me the jar and a spoon."

"Me, too."

Darla and Sally decided to wait. "What kind of food do they serve in Peru? It's not Mexican, is it?"

"Maybe. Do you think they serve lima beans in Lima, Peru?"

"That would be good, with a lot of ham."

"I'd rather have a hamburger. With onions and tomatoes."

"Mmmmmm. Sounds good."

"Yeah," Danny decided, around a mouthful of peanut butter. "It's boys' cook day, and we want to have hamburgers from a cafe while we're in town."

"If we go to a cafe, you have to cook later."

"Tomorrow is girls' day."

"No it isn't! Dad...?"

"That's enough, kids. We're going down now, and we'll settle the eating problem when we get there."

The hospital was easy to find due to the huge, painted white cross on its roof, and there was a lot of space in the parking lot to set down the chopper.

Two hours and many American hamburgers later, the chopper again climbed into the sky, heading for the top of the mountain and Lake Titicaca, now free of clouds.

"Will there be time to film before the sun gets too low?"

"If there isn't, can we spend the night on the island?"

"Does this temple have a sacrifice hole?"

"Dad?"

"Yes, Kitten?"

"I have a question. I heard one time that some tribes who made sacrifices to idols sometimes offered girls as a sacrifice. It isn't true, is it?"

There was silence from the front of the chopper.

"Is it, Uncle Monty?"

"There seems to be evidence that it happened."

"Like back at the leaning temple?"

"Possibly."

"But, Dad, why?"

"We don't know. Many religious cults have strange practices that do not seem to make sense. We believe that it is only the grace of God and our faith in Him that makes us acceptable for heaven. Some cults feel that if they do something that is hard to do or give up someone they love, like a daughter, their gods will favor them and maybe send rain for the crops. They feel that if they do something hard, their gods will love them for it. We feel that it is only the grace of God that makes our God love us, and no matter how good we are, it wouldn't be good enough without the grace of God."

"But why doesn't everyone feel like we do?"

"They would, if they believed in our God. But they seem to think they must DO something, rather than have faith that God has forgiven their sins."

"Is faith that hard to have?"

"You might ask Danny or Dennis. They were in a position to use their faith in their family to get them out of a problem, but the history professor had only God. He didn't know his prayers were being answered before he prayed by a God who put a thick cloud over Lake Titicaca, making us adjust our schedule."

"What if we had decided to wait for the cloud to go away?"

"We didn't, though. God has ways of making things happen."

The mountain was bathed in sunshine and was only a little bit cold. The boys still did not want to go swimming, though.

"Kitten, you and Sally will be taking the smaller camera, and I want you to get a lot of pictures of plants, trees and flowers. Also, shoot any insects or small animals you see. I don't think there is as much vegetation on the island as down with the temples, but watch out for snakes."

"Sure, Dad."

The sun shone brightly on the mountaintop, and Lake Titicaca and the contents of the island were put on film, then the "thwack, thwack, thwack" of the helicopter propeller carried them down to the valley temples.

"Dad, we want to spend the night in the brush shelter where the history teacher slept. Can we?"

"I think not. There may be snakes looking for a warm place to sleep. I would rather you be in the tent with a canvas floor to keep them out. It pays not to take chances."

"Aw, Dad...."

"No arguing, Dennis."

"But, Dad?"

"What, Kitten?"

"Do you think there may be some things the teacher left there? We could look. You know we didn't get to talk to him very long, and he wasn't feeling so good at the time."

"We could look."

The sun was very low when the helicopter again landed on the flat rock. Before opening the door, the photographer had words to say to his sons.

"Now, boys, just because we bought a longer rope, that doesn't mean you need to be exploring more holes. I don't want any of you to go ANYWHERE alone! Also, don't walk side by side. I don't want anyone slipping into anything, and two of you slipping would be even worse.

"Here's the plan. The girls will take the little camera and film every flower, vine and bush that looks interesting, and we'll add it to the ones they took at the lake. I want it done now, while the sun is low, and then again tomorrow, when the sun is overhead. We can use the ones we like best.

"Remember, it's still boys' turn to cook, so get busy on it. I will be working in the temples, but I have the walkie-talkie, and the boys will keep an open channel.

"Then, tomorrow, boys will do still shots of carvings, idols and whatever looks interesting. Girls will come with me. We should finish with the temples tomorrow. Darla will bring the recorder because we may need descriptive words recorded. Sally will carry one walkie-talkie, and you boys will carry the other, and you will keep it in your hand AT ALL TIMES. Understand?"

Four heads nodded soberly.

"Dad?"

"What, Danny?"

"How much extra time did you get from the government for bringing in the history teacher and having bad weather?"

"I asked for and got three more days. I think we'll need only two, but this way we have a cushion."

"Three days? I thought we would be through here tomorrow."

"We should, but I have another place to go."

"Where?"

"It's a surprise."

"A surprise! Why?"

"Because if I tell you, you might be so scared you wouldn't want to go, and if all four of you refused to go...."

"Aw, Dad...!"

"After a man-eating tiger, poison arrows and a sacrifice hole, what could be so bad?"

"You won't know until the day after tomorrow."

"Aw, Dad...."

"Boys, get busy with the cooking. Girls, take the camera and start shooting."

The girls went one way and the boys another, and Sally was heard to say, "I sure hope we have something good to eat."

Darla added, "Yeah, but with them, you never know."

An hour and a half later, the sun was gone, and everyone was dressed in their insulated coveralls, sipping hot chocolate. The corned beef hash for supper was good, hot and filling, and the mountainside was chilly from the wind blowing strongly up from the valley. Everyone was ready for sleep.

"Dad, I have a question."

"What is it, Kitten?"

"It's about faith. Dr. McConnell said he had faith that God would deliver him. When the boys were in the hole, they knew they had a way out, but when he fell in, he had no one. He didn't even know enough of the language to talk with his guides, and he thinks they got scared because they couldn't find him. What is faith?"

"Yeah, Uncle Monty. What is it? Does it mean the same as 'believing'?"

"Not exactly, Sally. The boys 'believed', because they 'knew' we were here. The doctor 'believed' because he had 'faith' in the promises of God. Faith is trusting someone so much that you know they cannot let you down, or knowing from past experience that promises will be kept. Who's ready with a verse?"

"I'm ready," offered Danny. "It's found in John 3:16. 'For God so loved the world that He gave His only Son, that whosoever believeth shall have everlasting life.' I think that kind of 'believing' is using faith."

"You're right. Next?"

"Me," offered Darla. "I remember when someone was sick, Jesus said, 'According to your faith, be it unto you'. I think if that person wasn't sure Jesus could heal him, he wouldn't have been healed."

"Good. Next?"

"I know one!" said Danny. "When Peter was permitted to walk on the water during the storm at sea, he looked around himself at the waves and lost faith. That made him start to sink, but Jesus held him up until his faith returned, and then he walked on the water to Jesus. I have a little bit of an idea how Peter felt. From down in the hole, it was hard to remember someone was going to pull me out."

"Fine. Sally?"

"Yes. 'I will give you rest.' Jesus said that, and I thought of it because I'm so tired I can hardly sit up."

"We all are, Sally. I like this one. 'A new commandment I give unto you, that ye love one another as I have loved you.' That sounds like we should love everyone, because that's what God does. Now, to bed with you before you go to sleep sitting there with your cocoa cups."

Twenty-four hours later, everyone was again dressed in their warm coveralls against the chilly night air. Devotions were over, and hot chocolate was gone.

"Into the chopper, girls. We have a big day tomorrow!"

"What are we doing, Dad?"

"It's a surprise, remember?"

"Aw, Dad...."

"We'd just as well go to sleep. Dad never changes his mind. Come on, Sally."

Sleep came quickly after the long, tired day of tramping through the bushes, vines and temple ruins. Then came the dawn. The monkeys began to bark and chatter, and the trees were alive with color.

Darla and Sally were startled awake by Dad's voice. "Hit the deck, girls. I have an assignment."

"Assignment? Already?"

"Right. Hear the birds in the trees? I want you to film as many of them as you can while the biscuits are cooking. Get a move on, now."

Biscuits and jelly concluded breakfast.

"I hoped we could find something the teacher left. Surely there would be something."

"I'll bet the monkeys got it, if there was."

"You're probably right. Boys, pack the stoves and food box. Girls, fold the tent and bedding. We move out in ten minutes."

"Just ten minutes?"

"Only nine and a half now."

Then the "thwack, thwack" of the propellers lifted the chopper out and up, and it began to climb toward the mountaintops.

"Back to the lake, Dad?"

"Wait and see."

"I'll bet it's a river, or something. Is it?"

"Wait and see."

"Aw, Dad...."

Mr. Jose Capito sat in the doorway of his stone and mud home in his little village. He wanted to be ready when the American came, and he had been waiting an hour when the "thwack, thwack" of the propeller blades signaled its arrival.

Strange request, it was, for a guide to lead the rich American around his village, and all the other places he wanted to go, and for that, he got good American dollars. He had many places to use his dollars. Clothes, glass windows for his home, and if there was enough, perhaps American paints for his little Juanita. She searched so hard for colors to use for her pictures, but berries and the red soil did not make all the colors she wanted, and, if possible, there might be paper... white paper... but all of that would wait.

The chopper swung over the small village, aiming toward a bare patch of ground.

"Oh, a village!"

"Is this it, Dad?"

"What fun! Look at all the people... and all the little kids. Who gets to take the pictures?"

"Will we be here all day?"

The helicopter stopped.

"Girls, take the small camera and film anything that interests you, being sure to get any plant or insect you don't already have. There is a girl named Juanita, and she is going to show you inside the houses. She knows no English, so you will just have to go where she takes you. Be sure to take enough pictures."

"Pictures of her, too?"

"Certainly. Boys will go with me. Juanita's father will be our guide, and he speaks some English. Sally, carry the walkie-talkie, and keep the channel open."

So the day began. Juanita shyly beckoned the girls to follow. She led them into her house where her mother sat on the floor, grinding a strange-looking kind of corn. The corn grains were blue, black and purple, instead of being all yellow. The ground cornmeal looked dirty, with all the colors mixed in, but the cakes made from it were yellow. Hmmm.

Juanita showed the girls where she slept. Against the walls was a stack of animal skins. Soft and fluffy, they seemed, and the girl took the top skin and shook it vigorously, making the fur stand up soft and fluffy. Then she covered it over with a colorful woven blanket made of wool. Smiling, she slipped under the blanket and lay down, closing her eyes. Darla snapped the shutter, and Juanita would sleep forever in the picture.

Laughing, she jumped up and smoothed the blanket, beckoning the girls to follow. She took them to the garden where squash, corn and pumpkins grew. One of the pumpkins had been cut open to expose the seeds. Juanita took a seed from the orange shell.

"Pepita."

"Pepita? Pumpkin seed?"

Juanita nodded excitedly and motioned the girls to follow. She led them through her mother's flowers and pointed to the tall sunflowers, then pointed to her mouth.

"Eat flowers?"

"Sally, she doesn't understand English."

Sally touched the sunflower petal, then her mouth, and Juanita shook her head and moved Sally's hand to the wide, seeded center.

"Oh, seeds? We eat sunflower seeds, too. Seeds?"

"Seeds?" repeated Juanita with a dimpled smile.

Through the village and down the street she led them, and many pictures later, they reached the village well, which wasn't a well. Water trickled from the side of the mountain and was caught in a rock-lined pool. Water spiders skated on top, but the water was so sparkling clear that tiny crawfish could be seen on the bottom. A gourd dipper lay on the rock nearby.

Juanita dipped some water and took a sip, her black eyes crinkled in a smile over the top of the gourd. Then she offered a drink to the girls.

They looked at each other in alarm. They had been instructed never to drink water from a strange place, so what would they do?

"Sally, pretend to drink. We don't want to hurt her feelings."

"Sure," and Sally put the dipper to her lips, then handed it to Darla.

For a long morning, they followed her, and it seemed that hours of shots were taken. Then Juanita pointed to the warm sun passing overhead and motioned them to follow her back to her home.

Dad and the boys were already there, watching Juanita's mother form strange-looking chunks of dough into floppy pancakes with her hands, which she slid into an iron kettle of bubbling oil. The cakes spit and sputtered, browning around the edges. With a long fork, she flipped the cakes over, and they continued browning.

From an open fire, she brought another deep iron kettle and set it beside the oil. She set a board beside the two kettles and, one by one, lifted the smoking and browned cakes to the board. With a long-handled spoon, she heaped a scoop of mixture onto each cake and set the board before her guests, smiling.

The mixture on the browned cakes seemed to be tomato, corn, beans and maybe squash or something, but whatever it was, it smelled wonderful. Juanita pointed to the food and to her mouth, then to Darla's and Sally's mouth. It was clearly an invitation to eat. Her father watched her, smiling with pride.

"My Juanita. Mama cooking good. She wants you eat. She have not words like me."

The girls lifted the crunchy cakes to their mouths, feeling that Juanita did very well without words. The spicy flavor was a bit startling but delicious, and the boys and Dad eagerly joined in. Mama smiled and formed more of the lumpy, floppy cakes and eased them into the bubbling oil. It would probably take a lot of them to fill everyone.

After lunch, Dad called them together. "Take off your boots and shake out your socks. Then lace them tight and get ready for a hike. A long hike."

"Where?"

"You'll see."

"The surprise, right?"

"You'll see."

Juanita waved as they left, following the guide on a path through trees and rocks. After two hours and two rest stops, they reached the mouth of a large, dark cave.

"This is the surprise, isn't it, Dad?"

"What's in there, lions or something?"

"Maybe cave birds?"

"I know! I know! It's bats!"

"Bats? Really?"

"A bat cave! Oh boy! Can I go in?"

"Wait," Dad cautioned. "We have to have a plan."

"But, Dad...."

"What, Kitten?"

"I always heard that bats land in people's hair. Especially girls' hair."

"Aw, Dad, that's just a superstition."

Dad nodded. "Maybe so, but we'll use these, just in case. Some superstitions are based on fact." With that, he pulled a handful of bandana scarves from his pocket. "Everyone put one on your head. If nothing more, it will keep your head clean."

"The plan, Dad?"

"All right. We will only get one chance at these pictures. Darla will stay out front and operate the movie camera. She WILL NOT BE SCARED AND RUN AWAY. She will HOLD TO THE CAMERA AT ALL TIMES, AIMING IT TOWARD THE MOUTH OF THE CAVE. Understand?"

"I can do it, Dad," offered Danny.

"No, she can do it. You will go with me."

"Inside the cave! Dennis, too! Really, Dad?"

"Yes. We have the low light film, and we will get as many shots as we can before the bats fly out."

"Oh, boy!"

"Uncle Monty, what do I do?"

"You have a very important job, Sally." With his knife, the photographer cut an armful of leafy branches. "You will stand directly behind Darla, and you will wave these branches around you. That should separate the stream of bats and keep them from flying directly at you and her and from the camera. Remember, we walked two hours to get to the cave for these pictures. We WILL GET GOOD PICTURES NO MATTER HOW NOISY AND SCARY IT GETS."

"Sure, Dad."

"I'm not afraid, Uncle Monty."

The scarves were tied over all heads, making everyone look like pirates. All they needed was a few eye patches! Darla was positioned twenty-five feet in front of the mouth of the cave, and Sally was behind her with her huge bouquet of leafy branches.

"Let's go, Dad!"

"Have patience, Dennis."

At the mouth of the cave, the boys began to creep inside. The darkness blinded them at first, then Dad turned on the infrared light, which would not disturb the bats but would allow pictures to be taken.

"Now, Danny," whispered Dad. "Follow my spotlight, and take pictures as fast as you can. Be careful, now, because the cave floor is slick with bat droppings."

"Droppings? Wheewww, yeah. I can smell them."

"They're getting on my shoes."

"Don't slide down, and DON'T drop the camera!"

Small, squeaky sounds came from the ceiling of the cave, and the spotlight revealed objects hanging like Christmas tree ornaments seemingly over every square inch of the cave roof. Here and there, one or two of them stretched their wings and squeaked.

"All right, Dan, get ready."

From his holster, Dad took the small snake pistol and aimed toward the rear of the cave.

"BANG!" went the shot, and in an instant, the cave was filled with black, moving objects, coming at them with arrow straightness. The flutter of wings past their heads was deafening, and words were useless.

Dennis yelled, "I WISH I HAD A CAMERA!"

From below him came a voice, "TAKE THIS ONE!"

"DANNY? WHERE ARE YOU?"

"DOWN HERE. I SLIPPED."

The red light located him, and the camera was transferred to Dennis, who was still standing.

"SNAP THE PICTURES FAST, SON," instructed Dad with a shout.

Dennis did.

Outside at the mouth of the cave, the girls heard the signal shot.

"Get ready," warned Sally.

"I'm rolling. I've got it propped on my knees, and I don't have any hands. You'll have to keep them off us."

Seconds after the shot, the bats began to pour out of the cave like a cloud of black gravy, flowing noisily overhead. The stream parted slightly to go around Sally's waving branches, but they came so close Darla could see their grinning faces and glittering eyes.

On and on came the black stream, and there was no question of running away scared. The girls were almost too frightened to move.

"Wave the branches!"

"I am! Fast as I can!"

"I wish they would shut up the squeaking! It makes me think of the book called *The Pied Piper of Hamlin*, where the piper was surrounded by squeaking mice and rats. These things even look like mice."

"Even worse! Mice with wings!"

The flow of black became thinner, and finally only a few straggling remnants came fluttering out. Then nothing.

Darla turned off the camera and watched the cave mouth.

"I hope Dad and the boys are all right."

"Here they come."

Dad held the gun and the spotlight, and Dennis held the camera. Behind them came Danny, walking strangely and holding out his hands away from his sides.

"Wheewww! What's that smell?"

"It's Danny. He fell in."

"Into what?"

"Bat poop!"

Dad corrected him. "Bat manure, called guano."

"Guano? Smells like poop."

The guide returned from his hiding place a safe distance away and led them to the return path.

"Danny, would you walk behind us?"

"But, Dad...?"

"Yes, son."

"Aw, Dad..." Walking behind may have been better for them, but it didn't help his own nose at all.

Two hours later, they entered the village. The sun was very low, and it was time to eat. Wonderful smells came from the house where Juanita lived.

Water was provided for Danny to bathe, and after a change of clothes, he smelled a lot better!

The girl motioned for Darla and Sally to follow. "Paint," she said.

"Paint?"

"She knows a word!"

"Paint," repeated Juanita, and she produced several sheets of paper. On it were pictures of birds and animals and small children. They were very good pictures. Very, very good pictures!

"Wait," instructed Darla and ran for her camera.

As Juanita displayed her paintings, Darla snapped pictures. These would be perfect for the documentary.

Spiced beans and corn cakes were set before them.

"Dad, Juanita is an artist. She paints."

The girl's father beamed and agreed, "Paints! Juanita wants colors. American dollars to buy paper and paint!"

"You're going to buy paints for her?"

"Could be money left for paints."

"Oh, Dad, can we send her some? We could pick out some really good ones, and she's been so nice to us all day. Would there be a way to get them to her from Missouri?"

Dad looked at the guide, who nodded. "Some weeks, packages come to our village. We have catalog? Picture book to buy things?"

"Oh, goodie, Dad! We can find good paints for her!"

"And some paper."

It was too late in the day to fly down the mountain, so the evening was spent in the chopper in the village square. Roosters crowed them awake before sunrise, and they lifted off the mountain, heading for Lima and a cafe breakfast.

Equipment was packed, and the camera gear was stowed into the jet.

"Beechking ICU2 to Lima Tower. Request permission to take off."

"Tower to Beechking ICU2...."

It was a weary family that set down at the Springfield, Missouri airport and transferred their gear to the van for the trip south to Branson.

Awaiting them was a letter from Phoenix, Arizona. Dad read it and put it aside.

"What did it say, Dad?"

"Well, the professor is fine after a good rest, and he would like a copy of our pictures from the temple ruins. His wife says we must get an assignment in Arizona and stay with them while we shoot it."

"Can we?"

"Perhaps. We'll see."

"I would like to see what Juanita paints on the paper and paints we send her."

"I wish I could paint."

"Have you tried?"

"Yes."

"Well, we took good pictures, and you were brave when you kept the bats off our heads."

"That's me," agreed Sally. "I'm a good bat batter."

"Did we leave Danny's clothes in Peru?"

"Yes, and I hope they buried them."

"What's in Arizona that we could film?"

"Dad'll find something."

After much cutting away and rearranging, the film from the temple ruins was put together and fitted with the words and music that would make it interesting. The idol stood with outstretched arms, and Danny whispered, "Don't look at him, Dennis. He just wants to get us down in that hole again."

Then came long shots of the dark mouth of the bat cave. There was nothing moving for a long, tense moment, then out streamed the flying mammals. Sally and Darla ducked, involuntarily, as the mouse-faced bats streamed out of the cave. It was even more frightening to see them in the film, because the girls kept their eyes open.

Darla whispered, "How did you keep from running away when those things came at us?"

"I shut my eyes."

"You did? So did I!"

"But I like the pictures we took a lot better. Juanita is so pretty in the pictures, and she looked right into the camera and smiled like a movie star. And I love all the flowers and vines. We can show that one when the company figures out the names of all of them. We have Juanita's address, and we can send her a picture of herself."

"You know what I've decided?"

"What?"

"I'm going to take photography in school. I think films like we made would help me get a good grade."

"I guess it wouldn't be cheating, because your dad's a professional photographer."

"Nope! We took the pictures. All we have to do is learn how to put them together without the edges showing and being on top of each other."

"Uncle Monty can show us."

"Then why bother to take it in school?"

"You're right. Let's take cooking instead."

"Yeah. Let's."

"Even better, we could figure a way to make the boys go! Their cooking could use a little help."

"Do you really think so?"

FOOTSTEPS IN THE CANYON

BOOK 3
BURIED TREASURE
&
STRANDED

BURIED TREASURE

Too much work! Thirteen-year-old Caitlyn Bradford stood up to rest her back. Rivulets of perspiration gathered on her forehead and flowed down into her eyes, and the salt of her sweat caused her eyes to burn and sting. She drew the sleeve of her work shirt across her face and sighed. The sun beat down unmercifully onto the rows of green beans that stretched out before her.

At the next garden row beside her, ten-year-old Nelda commented. "Sweat in the eyes stings, doesn't it? I think we need windshield wipers for our sweat to keep it out of our eyes so we can see."

"Good idea. Let me know where to get some."

Caitlyn stooped down again and felt among the stickery bean vines, searching with her fingers for the clusters of green beans. Giving the handful of ripe beans a tug, she tossed them into the basket. The first part of June was not quite so hot as July and August, but the humidity of the garden caused a lot of sweat anyway.

"Do we have to pick them all today?" Nelda asked, fully knowing the answer.

"Yeah, because there'll be something else that has to be picked tomorrow. Blackeye peas, corn or more tomatoes."

Nelda wiped her own face and slapped at the cluster of buzzing gnats determined to fly into her eyes.

"Cat...?"

"What?"

"What if we wore glasses... maybe something like welding goggles that had sides on them? It might keep the gnats away."

Caitlyn thought a minute. "Worth a try. You know how we invented wearing rain slickers to pick okra to keep off the itchy fuzz. I'd think we could get some safety glasses that would fit us."

"But not right now, huh?"

"You're right. No time."

They moved along in silence as the pile of beans in the basket neared the top. Another few minutes, and they would be through with this patch.

Caitlyn stood and rubbed her aching back while she studied the rows of bean vines. "Nellie? Would you rather we pull the vines now and do the corn later? Or get the corn now and pull the vines this evening?"

After a moment of thought, Nelda had an answer. "Let's do the dusty old vines now while we're already itchy and then jump in the stock tank to get rid of the dirt."

"You got it! Why don't you start pulling the vines, and I'll take these beans in, and then bring back the tractor?"

"Got it."

Caitlyn hoisted the basket of beans onto her hip and carried it to the end of the row. Plopping the basket into the trailer, she turned the key in the tractor ignition switch.

At the "But-ut-ut" of the engine, she stepped on the gas and turned the wheel. The small garden tractor headed, noisily, for the ranch house. When she returned, her twin brother, Cal, was riding in the trailer.

"He's going to haul the vines in for us. With both of us pulling, it'll be quick. Then he's going to replant. Mom wants us to get the tomatoes next. It'll be corn tomorrow."

Nelda sighed and grumbled, "Everything has to be done today."

"Yeah, today and tomorrow. It's partly on account of what we've got next week."

"Too many guests, you mean?"

Caitlyn nodded, over her armload of dusty bean vines. "We've got the archeological class, the bird watchers, the day party for someone's birthday, and…."

"I know. The archery club that's going to have to sleep in the stable loft."

"Right. Maybe there's someone else. I don't really remember."

The tomato vines were loaded to the breaking point with the tasty scarlet globes, and the two girls pulled the reddest ones, placing them carefully in the shallow basket. These would be stored in the icehouse for salads. Then, next would come those larger tomatoes to be sliced and put in the sundryer for soups and sauces.

Caitlyn commented, "Look at all the green ones. I'll bet we'll be picking them next week to make sweet pickle relish."

Nelda agreed. "Good. We don't have to be so careful with them."

An hour later, they tossed off their hats and sandals and jumped into the cool water of the stock tank. A few splashes and a few quick duck-unders, and they were back in the garden, soggy, dripping and a little bit cooler.

In and out of the vegetable patch every day! It would be this way of it for the most of June.

In a town some distance away another girl of thirteen and a half, impatiently dragged the comb through her glossy, black hair. Her brown eyes were half-hidden by her deep frown, and her well-shaped mouth was set in a firm line. There were times when everything went wrong.

Here it was, the month of June, and school was out. She should be having fun with her best friend, but, instead, she was being dumped. Not only that, but the place where she was being dumped didn't have room for her and really didn't want her.

Mom was on the telephone with the hospital in Topeka, Kansas, checking on Grandma's condition.

"Tomorrow? Oh, my, that soon! Well... I can try. I might be there by evening... if I can get a flight right away... yes, thank you." She hung up and turned toward the girl.

"I have to go right now. Grandma is being released today."

"But if you can't get there to take her home...?"

"Well, I guess... Well, we'll see. Are you packed?"

"Packed for what? I was packed to go to Marcie's house, but how does a person pack to be shipped to the country?"

Mom sighed. "I don't know, darling. Things are not going according to plan. I did not plan to take care of Grandma this week, but it turns out that I have to. You can't go to Marcie's house with her in the hospital. Who would know that her appendix would rupture?"

"I could stay here...."

"No. It is not safe for a girl your age to stay alone. With Dad on the road and your brother having to go on that practice dig...."

"But it's only a practice dig...."

"Don't argue. I know that, but he must go to the practice dig, or he can't go to Mexico. We've put too much money and time into this course for him to risk a bad grade."

"I could stay in the house the whole time and not stick my head out. We could have enough food and...well, maybe I could...."

For a minute Mom seemed to be considering the suggestion, and then she shook her head. "No. It wouldn't be safe."

"Could I go with you?"

"No, darling. I'm sorry, but it's just not a place for you to be, and I won't have any time to be with you. The only thing to do is go to the country with your brother."

"But, Mom, the college girls don't want me along, and I can't stay in the bunkhouse with Matthew. There's not even room to sleep on the floor with ten other girls to the cabin. I know they're being nice to say I can come, but I hate to be unwanted."

Mom sighed. "I know, darling. But I have to get ready to go, and you don't have a choice. Sometimes we just have to accept help. You will know how to stay out of the way of the other girls. Maybe you can find a way to help them. Everyone has troubles sometimes, and ours are now. So pack up, and do the best you can. Say, maybe you should call one of the girls and ask what they pack."

"Aw, Mom, I hate to bother them. How can I be wrong with jeans and tee shirts?"

Her college brother, Matthew, came in at that moment, and the door banged behind him. "And put in a straw hat, your swimsuit, and track shoes."

"Swimsuit...?"

"Yeah. There's a little river that flows beside the dig site. As hot as it is, I'd think there would be a lot of swimming."

"Swmming? Well, I think..."

Whereupon, Mom had something to say. "But Matthew... swimming in a river? I really don't think...."

"Aw, Mom, remember all those expensive swimming lessons she's had?"

"Of course. But, still...."

"Tell you what I'll do, Mom. I'll drive a stake in the ground and tie a rope to it. I'll tie the other end around her waist. That way I can just pull her out when she's about to drown."

The girl looked from her Mom to her brother and back, and the whole idea of her being tied to the bank was suddenly funny. Mom grinned and finally made up her mind.

"All right. But remember, Miss Gwinneth Marie Copeland, if you fall in the river and get yourself drowned, I'll never forgive you!"

Gwinnie knew that when Mom laughed, the battle was over. She also knew that when she was called Gwinneth Marie Copeland, her mother absolutely meant what she said. The best thing to do now, of course, was to give Mom a hug and keep her own mouth shut. Which she did.

"I'll go get packed, now, Mom, so I can ride to the airport with you."

It was three days later that Gwinnie Copeland stood with her brother, ready to board the chartered bus to the country. It was jam packed full of excited college students… yelling guys and laughing girls… all of them at least five years older than Gwinnie.

She squenched herself into the corner of the bench along the back of the bus, trying to take up as little space as possible. She stared at her folded hands in her lap and tried not to think about how awful it would be when they got to where they were going.

Ahead of her, she still had the embarrassing problem of trying to disappear when they got to the cabin. There was a bit of discussion as to the smallness of the cabin. It seemed there would be no floor space, even, to put her bedroll. She thought about offering to sleep in the closet or under the bed…or maybe in the shower stall. It was terrible to be not wanted.

After the ride of about an hour, the bus bumped off onto another road that wound around the little hills and groves of trees.

"There it is! I see it!"

"Yeah! Look at it! The BB Ranch!"

"What's the "BB" for?"

"Beats me. Maybe Buried Bones."

"I see a cow!"

"That isn't a cow…it's a bull."

"Isn't a bull a cow?"

"No, it's a male bovine."

"All right, the BB stands for Bad Bovine."

"Or Beautiful Bovine."

"I like Buried Bones better."

And at that time they pulled under the wide iron gates and the ranch house was just ahead. Behind it was a tall barn, a windmill by the stock watering tank, and piles of hay bales were everywhere. There was a long bunkhouse and three guest cabins. Parked by the bunkhouse were several cars, pickup trucks, and a pop-up travel trailer.

The bus, being driven by one of the sponsors, pulled into the space between two of the cabins.

"Everybody out!"

Groan, groan! The moment Gwinnie dreaded was upon her.

IDEA! Maybe they'd let her sleep in the bus! Probably not. She huddled back in her corner and let everyone else get off before her. Finally, she could put it off no longer. Picking up her suitcase, she followed along behind the fellow with a camera and binoculars hanging around his neck.

Mr. Bradford was busy in the ranch bunkhouse, and Mrs. Bradford was in the middle of making tomato juice, and it was very messy. That was why Caitlyn was standing by Guest Cabin One to see if anything was needed.

Loud and laughing college girls in cutoff jeans and faded tee shirts filed past her, ignoring her just as if she was part of the scenery. That was just fine with Caitlyn. She had plenty to do without answering complaints about towels and soap.

The fellows from the bus trailed away behind Cal, Caitlyn's twin brother, as he led them to the bunkhouse. The girls all filed into the guest cabin. Caitlyn followed the last girl.

"If there's anything you need..." she offered.

One of the sponsors swung open the bathroom door. "Let's see...soap, towels...tissue.... Nope, we don't need a thing. Thanks." And with that, Caitlyn was dismissed.

Smiling to herself over her good fortune, Caitlyn eased out the door and bumped squarely into one last girl.

GIRL! Where did this one come from? She was so young! Why, she couldn't be more than fourteen…maybe fifteen, at the oldest. No…she was more like thirteen.

"Are you…?"

The girl tightened her lips and frowned slightly. "I'm afraid I am."

Caitlyn still stared at the girl.

"Did I do something wrong?" the girl asked her.

"Oh, no! I'm sorry. I didn't mean to stare. It's just that…."

"Just that what…?"

"You seem so young to be in college! You must be terribly smart…or maybe you're older than you look. Oh, forgive me! I'm stuttering and making a fool of myself. And it's none of my business."

The girl stepped back out of the cabin and put her suitcase on the ground. "No, you're not making a fool of yourself. I'm not in college. I just got sent along with these people like a piece of baggage. Do you live here…I mean are you a part of the ranch?"

Caitlyn grinned, as she thought of all the work she and Nelda had done in the past week. "Yes, I'm part of this. I'm the workhorse!"

"You're the…? Oh, I see! You're funny! Hey, maybe you could help me."

"With what?"

"Could you tell me, is there a laundry house, a shed or some place where I could sleep?"

"You don't like the cabin?"

"Oh, I'm sure it's nice, but there isn't room for me. I got pushed into this because my family came apart all at once and there was no place for me to be. My brother has the money to give to someone to keep me, but of course I can't stay in the bunk house with him."

"You're not in college….not part of the diggers?"

"I'm thirteen, going on thirteen and a half. I have to stay here and be in everybody's way for all three days of the dig. Hey, maybe I could sleep in the lunchroom. Do you think…?"

- END OF EXCERPT -

ADDITIONAL BOOK SERIES BY JOANN KLUSMEYER

The Great I Am Bible Story Series for Kids
6 books

The Young Pioneers Adventure Series for Kids
5 books

The Wentworth Triplets Mystery Series for Young Teens
3 books

Footsteps in the Canyon Adventure Series for Young Teens
4 books

Burnt Tree Junction Historical Fiction Series for Adults
6 books

Ozark Mountains Historical Fiction Series for Adults
7 books

Taming the Wilderness Historical Fiction Series for Adults
4 books

The Sheltering Stone Historical Fiction Series for Adults
5 books

The Trilogy of Wishbone Hollow Historicial Fiction Series for Adults
3 books

www.ingramcontent.com/pod-product-compliance
Lightning Source LLC
Chambersburg PA
CBHW060839250626
47162CB00005B/2113

* 9 7 8 1 6 1 3 1 4 6 5 6 9 *